Echo of Choices

Shavona White

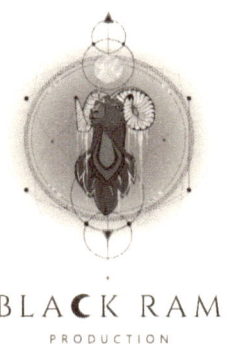

BLACK RAM
PRODUCTION

Black Ram Production, United States

TABLE OF CONTENTS

The book is for my husband, S. S. White
To the sun, moon, stars, to forever!

GRAY NO COLOR

Anna woke before her alarm clock went off, but she decided to keep her eyes closed for a bit longer. She dreaded getting up and facing her husband's disappointment. Her children had seemed genuine when they'd told her she'd get the next job, but Robert had not been so kind. He'd questioned her about the interview: what their demeanor was like, what questions they asked, how she responded. Hell, she'd asked herself those same questions to try to figure out what went wrong, but dwelling on them hadn't changed anything. She'd still received the rejection letter in the mail.

The letter was on parchment paper the color of eggshells. The rough feeling of it reminded her of sand stuck between toes. She knew the two sentences by heart.

Dear Mrs. Jacobs,

We regret to inform you we will be going with another candidate. We want to thank you for your consideration of us.

S. Whitehead
CEO, G.R.E.R.S.

So simple and to the point. Anna had worked hard to get the interview; she networked her ass off for three months before even applying and had thought she had it in the bag. Yet she'd failed. She recalled the conversation she'd had the previous night with her husband while he was driving home. She hated talking to him on speakerphone. He always sounded like he was preaching to her, like he had an audience.

His voice carried a high pitch of desperation. "Anna, money is tight. Our savings can't withstand you being unemployed."

She already knew that, of course, but she also knew he had to get it off his mind. Robert wasn't the kind of person to hold back. And God forbid their savings dip below six figures.

"Anna, I'm sorry, but you're going to have to bite the bullet and take the job with the hydration company. I know it's not what you wanted, but our family's needs come first."

Anna remembered feeling angry, but she couldn't remember her reply. She couldn't remember serving the children dinner. She couldn't remember anything, for that matter. She wondered if she'd been drinking, but nothing came to mind. The last memory she had was of Robert berating her.

She turned over in bed to wake him, but she could feel he wasn't there. It surprised her. In the ten years they'd been married, her husband had never gotten up before her. She opened her eyes.

Instead of Robert, another man was sitting on a cot nearby. She shot upright, startled, and yelled, "Who the fuck are you?"

The sudden motion made her light-headed. Her heart beat fast, and the hairs on her arms stood on end. She looked around. To her horror, she wasn't in her bed. She didn't know where she was. It was an all-gray room with two cots, one for her and one for him. There were no windows. The floor was shiny, a hard yet smooth wax. She found an opening for a door, but there was no door connected to it.

She turned back to the man, afraid to take her eyes off him for too long. He appeared to be in his late forties and wore a gray linen shirt with matching pants. His jet-black hair was disheveled and greasy, and he was thin with hollowed-out cheeks, as if he'd missed several meals. But the most prominent feature was his eyes. They were dark and piercingly large. They scared the shit out of her.

"Hello?" she asked. "Did you hear me? Who are you?"

He just stared at her. Anna grew frustrated, still anxious because she didn't know where she was. When she realized nothing was keeping her in the room, she stood to leave. It was then she noticed she was wearing the same gray outfit as Mr. Skinny Face. *Who the fuck changed my clothes?* she thought.

From beyond the door, a man yelled, "Where am I? And who are you, and how'd you get me here?" Anna could tell he was from the South because his accent was thick and ignorant. From the sound of it, he was just as frightened as she was.

Another man yelled in pain. "Stop! How dare you raise your hand to me. I didn't bring you here. I just woke up, the same as you."

Anna needed to find out what was going on. All she knew was she'd been kidnapped, and she wasn't the only one. It didn't seem like Mr. Skinny Face would be any help, so she went through the doorway alone. She emerged into a large circular room that held lush gray couches with matching pillows. Every wall was gray. There were no windows, but in the ceiling were small holes of light about every five feet. More doors off the main room led to a kitchen and other rooms. It was the creepiest house she'd ever been in.

The Southern man's voice came from an open doorway. "Hey, boy. What's wrong with your eyes? You sick or something?"

"Pardon?" the other man spat. "What do you mean? There's nothing wrong with my eyes. And I am not your boy."

Anna decided the ignorant man's nickname would be Southern Delight. Nicknaming people was one of the ways she remembered who was who when she was in large groups. It had come in handy at her last job.

She approached the doorway and found a room like the one she'd left. Southern Delight turned out to be a thin White man with short hair, wearing the same gray outfit as her. He stood by one of the cots, hunched over as if his back were broken and squirting at the other gentleman in the room.

Whoa. Anna immediately nicknamed the guy Mr. Gorgeous. Although he was sitting on his cot, Anna could tell he was tall and muscular. He was Asian with an outgrown mohawk, the craziest hairstyle she had seen in a while. But the color was what intrigued her—silver, like metallic water.

When she walked in, they looked at her. Southern Delight cleared his throat, stood up straight, and said, "Well, hello, ma'am. Do you happen to know what's going on around here?"

Anna eyed both of them. "No, I don't. I think we were kidnapped and brought here, but I don't know why."

A scream pierced the air. Mr. Gorgeous jumped off his bed, and they all ran toward the sound. In another room identical to theirs, a Hispanic woman stood over a sleeping Black woman.

When the first woman saw them, she steadied herself, wiping her hands down her shirt and taking a deep breath. "I woke up and noticed her. I tried to wake her, but she's not responding."

Mr. Gorgeous knelt beside the sleeping woman and checked her pulse. Anna assumed he had medical experience and waited for his prognosis.

The Hispanic woman studied each of them. "I guess we're all in the same situation, since we're wearing the same outfit."

Mr. Gorgeous finished examining the woman and stood. "She seems fine. Just not responsive."

Anna was at a loss for words. She was scared, and a million thoughts raced through her mind. Where was she? Who had brought her there? Was there a ransom for her? But she was more worried about her children. Were they okay? She couldn't remember anything except the conversation with her husband, then waking up in that strange room.

"Who cares about some damned nigger?" asked Southern Delight.

The crude remark pulled Anna from her thoughts. She couldn't believe her ears. She knew some people were prejudiced, but she'd never heard anyone just come right out and say something like that.

The Hispanic woman turned to him, a look on her face as though she'd sucked a lemon. "How dare you. Who do you think you are, asshole?"

Southern Delight pointed his finger at her face. "Now, you listen here, woman. You ain't gon' stand here and disrespect me that way. Who do you think *you* are? I ought to whip your—"

The Hispanic woman was about to speak when they heard a shuffling sound at the door. Anna turned and was shocked to see three little boys, no older than five, standing in the open doorway. One of the boys was watching the adults through narrowed eyes. The other two were huddled close together, keeping their distance from him.

Anna put her hands up to indicate the others should be quiet and said, "Okay, now listen, everyone. We're all confused. Let's go sit in the common room and discuss this."

They left the room and moved to the gray couches. Anna assessed the boys. After they sat down, she knelt in front of them so they could see she meant no harm.

"Hello, fellas. My name is Anna."

She wanted to take it slow with them, but Mr. Gorgeous said, "Thank you for that, Anna, but before we get to the children, let's introduce ourselves." He inclined his head at something behind her. She turned and saw Mr. Skinny Face staring at them from across the room.

"Oh, yes," she said. "He was in the room with me. He doesn't say much."

Mr. Gorgeous nodded. "Well, except for the boys, we're all adults, and we'll discuss what's happening together. Cure, please join us."

"I'm sorry, did you call him 'cure'?" Anna asked, confused by the term. "Do you know him?"

Mr. Gorgeous looked confused too, like he didn't understand her question. "No."

Mr. Skinny Face slowly made his way to the common room. All eyes were on him. When he reached them, he said in a dull voice, "Hello. I have searched the entire place, and there's no way out. I've come to the conclusion we're all dead."

That did it for Southern Delight. "Oh, enough with that. No, we ain't dead. And since I'm the only White man here, I ought to be in charge."

"Excuse me?" the Hispanic woman asked.

Southern Delight spoke over her. "I'll start. My name is Jim Green, and I'm the overseer of the Moore Holmes Plantation of Alabama. The next person to speak will be Anna."

The Hispanic lady glared at him. Anna couldn't believe how highly Southern Delight thought of himself. She imagined he was one of the sick bastards who voted to restrict other people's rights.

She searched everyone's eyes before she spoke. She couldn't understand why they were all so calm. A dreadful question kept circulating in her mind: where were her children?

"Okay," she said. "Thank you, Mr. Green. My name is Anna Jacobs. I am a wife and mother of two, and I'm unemployed at the moment." She wasn't sure she should have said the last part. She wanted everyone to take her seriously.

"Well, thank you, ma'am," Mr. Green said. "As we are the only civil folk here—"

Mr. Gorgeous cut him off. "Okay, look, cure. I'm not sure what your issue is, but if you say one more word that's an injustice, well, let's just say you'll be sorry. Do you understand?"

The two started to argue, but the Hispanic woman snapped her fingers. The sound was piercing and effective. Both men fell quiet.

"Let's stop the dick-waving contest here," she said. "Did any of you hear what he said? There are no doors or windows. I don't care who you guys are. The real questions are how did we get here and what's going on? I need answers."

No one said a word.

After a moment, Mr. Gorgeous said, "I'm going to search the house." He stalked out while everyone else remained frozen. Anna was happy someone finally seemed as panicked as she was. She hoped Mr. Skinny Face was wrong. Maybe he'd missed something.

She heard Mr. Gorgeous curse as he made his way around the house. When he returned to them, there was defeat on his face.

"He's right." He looked around at everyone. "We need to figure this out. The last thing I remember is getting into my own bed. I don't remember falling asleep, just waking up here. My name is Ian Chen. I live in section 42-56." The others seemed at a loss for words, so he asked, "Why the strange faces?"

"What or where is section 42-56?" Anna asked.

He rolled his eyes. "In New China. District 42, section 56?"

Anna hadn't done well in geography, but she was pretty sure there wasn't a place called New China.

"I knew something was wrong with you," Mr. Green said. "Not even an American."

Before they could start bickering again, the Hispanic woman held her hand up. "I want to try something." She fixed Ian and Mr. Green with a steely glare. "I'm going to ask each of you a question. Just humor me and answer, okay?"

They nodded. Anna admired the woman for taking control. She held herself high, like she didn't want to seem like a little housewife.

"Mr. Green, sir," the woman said, "who is the president of the United States?"

Anna was puzzled by why she would ask such a simple question, like she was talking down to him. It angered Anna a little even though the man deserved it.

"Lady, the president is James Madison," Mr. Green said.

The Hispanic woman flinched in surprise. Anna couldn't believe her ears. Was the man crazy?

Ian started to say something, but the woman held her hand up again. "Thank you, Mr. Green. Ian, please be patient. My name is Linda Hernandez. I'm the president of a manufacturing plant for Shaz Soda. Can you answer one question for me?"

Ian looked perplexed but nodded.

"What year is it?" she asked.

Anna's heart was beating beyond its boundaries. She wished she knew where the questions were going.

Ian seemed to understand. "For me, it's the year 2140."

They let his answer sink in.

Mr. Skinny Face broke the silence. "Very interesting." All eyes moved to him. He wasn't looking at them but at the large gray table between the couches. On it were words Anna didn't recognize, written in large black letters.

Unus puer habet muri. Prudenter elige.

"What does it say?" Linda asked.

Anna didn't give a shit what it said. Had they not heard Ian? What did he mean it was the year 2140?

Mr. Skinny Face didn't answer. Instead, he considered the boys. The two who seemed more timid looked away, but the third stared back at him.

Linda broke the silence. "Okay, so Ian is from 2140, and it seems Mr. Green is from the 1800s. Is that correct, sir?"

Mr. Green frowned. "Well, yes. The year is 1815. But I don't understand. You said you're a president? In what country?"

Linda shook her head. "I'm the president of a major corporation in the USA in the year 2025. I know it must be hard for you to believe, but a lot changes from 1815 to my time. Slavery was dead long before I was born, and the president of the United States is a Black woman."

Mr. Green scoffed but didn't say a word. Linda continued. "Anna, what year is it for you?"

Anna looked at each of them. She still didn't understand why they were so calm. Were they saying they were all from different times? She wasn't sure she believed them, but she couldn't deny Mr. Green's ignorance.

She decided to keep her reply simple. "For me, it's 2017."

Mr. Skinny Face suddenly walked over to the three boys. "Hello," he said. "What are your names?" He pointed to each one.

The first boy said, "Lorenzo." He was thinner than the others, with long sandy hair. He seemed curious, observing everyone with an inquisitive expression.

The boy who hadn't been afraid spoke next. "Donny." He had a scar on his forehead and a large nose. The cold way he regarded everyone scared Anna.

The third, a small boy with black hair, said, "Snkt."

Anna frowned. Could he be Snkt Khet, the dictator responsible for the deaths of millions of Muslim people, or just a boy with the same name? Mr. Skinny Face met her gaze, and she knew he was wondering the same thing.

He turned back to the boys. "Thank you. Can you be good lads and go back to your room?"

"I don't want to," Donny said, his voice hard.

It surprised Anna. He couldn't be more than five, but he seemed older. The others were at a loss for words, too.

"Please," Anna said.

The boy glared at her. "No. I don't have to listen to you."

"Go," Ian commanded.

Donny stood and stomped off to one of the open doorways across the room. The other two boys looked to Anna, as if for direction, so she indicated it was okay.

When the boys were back in their room, Ian, who had his eyes on Mr. Skinny Face, said, "Okay, cure. What does the writing say? I know you understand it."

Mr. Skinny Face paced back and forth in thought. He didn't seem to have heard Ian.

"What is 'cure'?" Anna asked again.

Like before, Ian seemed puzzled. Then his expression cleared. "I forgot you're not from my time. It's just a casual way to address someone."

Mr. Skinny Face suddenly crossed the room and strode out to the kitchen. They heard the refrigerator door open, then the clatter of dishes on a countertop. The others followed and found him taking hasty bites of bread, meats, and cheese without finishing any of it. He barely swallowed before moving on to the next.

As they watched him, Anna had a feeling she knew what time period he was from. "Sir," she said softly. "Are you from the 1930s?"

Linda sucked in a breath that told Anna she understood as well and said, "Let's give him some time." She directed everyone back to the common room.

After they returned to the sofas, Mr. Green broke the silence. "Well, if I'm to believe any of this nonsense, it seems I'm at a disadvantage here. I know my ancestry, but you're all beyond my time. Can someone explain what the devil is going on with that man in the kitchen?"

Anna thought that was the brightest thing he'd said all day.

Linda answered. "In the 1930s, a cruel man in Egypt, a man who hated religion and wanted to abolish it, slaughtered millions of Sunni Muslims. It was called the Muslim Purge. Those who weren't killed were taken to camps or went into hiding." She gestured toward the kitchen. "We think he was in the middle of that before he woke up here."

Ian said, "I remember learning something about that, but I don't know a lot of details."

Linda gave them a brief summary of the war. To Anna's surprise, she didn't refer to Snkt Khet by name. When Linda finished, Ian looked horrified.

Mr. Green appeared to be deep in thought. He looked a little sick, like Ian, but he didn't comment on the war. Instead, he turned to Anna. "Ma'am, what happens to the White man? Why are colored women the presidents of companies and niggers the presidents of our great nation?"

"Don't call them that," Linda said.

Anna wasn't sure how to answer. She didn't like Mr. Green grouping her with him, like they shared the same beliefs just because they were White. But she thought it showed progress that he hadn't tried to argue with Linda. "Well, Mr. Green," Anna said, "over time, White people learn to be more tolerant. They understand we're all humans, and in America, we try to be civil to each other."

Linda laughed humorlessly and turned to Ian. "What happened in China?"

Ian looked at Mr. Green, then at Anna, and said, "Nothing happened in China itself. Anna just suggested the so-called White man learns from his mistakes, but that's not the case. America as a whole never got it together. Your country was so far in debt it collapsed. China came in and took what was hers. The US is now New China."

Everyone let that sink in. Anna was beyond confused and scared of what the future held. She wanted to figure out what was going on. "Okay," she said. "Let's think this through. Why are we here? Why us? We must have something in common with each other."

But as she spoke, she eyed Mr. Green and couldn't think of a single thing they might have in common aside from their skin color. He was a racist, and she didn't want to think about the horrible things he was doing to the Black people on his plantation.

The others seemed stumped too. They all stared at each other.

Anna continued. "Okay, what we know so far is that Mr. Green is from 1815, the gentleman in the kitchen the 1930s, I'm from 2017, Linda 2025, and Ian 2140. We don't know anything about the woman on the cot or the boys, so I suggest we start there."

Everyone nodded. Anna stood to make her way to the boys' room, just as Mr. Skinny Face returned from the kitchen. He grabbed her arm to stop her. "Wait," he said. "That boy."

Anna knew he was talking about Snkt and understood why he wouldn't want her to speak with him, but his intense expression unnerved her. When she tried to free herself, he shook his head.

That seemed to piss Mr. Green off. He moved with lightning speed toward Anna. "Now, you look here," he spat. "Ain't no one going to mishandle a White woman in my presence. I don't care where you are from!"

The three of them stood there scowling at each other, waiting for someone to make a move. Ian just watched them.

Linda, however, started pacing and said, as if to herself, "God, grant me the serenity to accept the things I cannot change, the courage to change the things I can, and the wisdom to know the difference."

Her words broke the tension. Mr. Skinny Face let go of Anna and gestured for everyone to go back to the sitting area.

As they returned to the couches, he asked Linda, "Do you believe what you just said?"

"Of course I do. Why?"

Mr. Skinny Face sat and appeared to gather his resolve before speaking. "My name is Mostafa. I don't understand how this is happening. I was taken to a prison camp in the desert and was waiting to die before I woke up here. I do not know if my wife or children are still alive. I have witnessed the slaughter of my neighbors and the heinous acts of the devil himself. You're from the future. I must know, do my people make it? Who wins the war?"

Linda and Anna exchanged wary glances. Anna decided to let her answer.

"Yes and no," Linda said. "The number of deaths was never known exactly; it's between five and six million. The war was won, but your culture was devastated. In time, it built itself from the ashes, but from what we heard from Ian, I don't know if any of it matters."

Mostafa listened, deep in thought. "Well, if what you said is true, about having the courage to change things, it all matters. It all matters."

"Well, Mostafa, can you please enlighten us?" Ian asked impatiently. "So we're all on the same level."

Mostafa took a deep breath. "I am a broken man, but it seems fate has given us a chance to fix what is broken." He pointed to the words etched on the table. "What is written there is Latin. 'One child has to die. Choose wisely.'" He let that sink in, then continued. "If I understand correctly, I have the chance to change history. Because I believe one of those boys is the devil himself. The tyrant Snkt Khet."

The room fell eerily quiet. Mr. Green gawked at everyone. Finally, he asked, "What kind of world are we in that we kill White children? I won't be a part of this."

Mostafa looked angry. "How dare you talk about White children. I know all about the dealings in America. How you treat your Black people. You enslave them as my people are enslaved. You treat them as if they were not human. You are as bad as Khet. I would kill a hundred White children for the chance to save my family. It seems Allah has given us the opportunity to right a wrong."

Mr. Green seemed struck silent. There was something in his expression Anna hadn't seen from him yet. Sympathy or guilt. She wondered if speaking on an even level with the kind of people he normally considered beneath him was making him rethink his principles.

It was Linda who piped up. "Mostafa, I understand, but we must do our due diligence and make sure. We need to find out who the other two boys are. Because I don't think it'll be an easy choice for us to make."

Ian went to retrieve the children from their room. Everyone watched as he marched them over. Until she saw them again, Anna hadn't registered she was going to have to choose to kill two of them. She wondered if the boys had overheard the conversation or understood what was happening. An awful thought occurred to her: would she and the others have to do it themselves?

Ian sat the boys down, then nodded at Anna. "Hello," she said, her voice shaking. "I'm going to ask you boys some questions. Try your best to answer, okay? We'll start with Snkt. Do you understand what I'm saying?"

Snkt didn't answer. Anna gestured at Mostafa. When he repeated the question in Arabic, the boy nodded.

"Okay," Anna said. "How old are you?"

Mostafa translated, and Snkt put five stubby fingers in the air.

"Thank you," Anna said. "Do you know your full name?"

Mostafa asked in Arabic, and the boy nodded.

Anna grew impatient. "Could you please say it out loud?"

After Mostafa translated, the boy said, "Snkt Khet," followed by something Anna didn't understand. She waited expectantly for Mostafa to fill in the blanks, but he jumped to his feet.

He pointed at the boy and snarled, "I knew it. There is no more discussion."

"Mostafa," Anna hissed. "Contain yourself. I understand, but you have to see, these are boys, not men." She wasn't inclined to share it with the group, but she didn't know if she'd be able to harm the children, no matter who they were. "What did he say?"

Mostafa was still fuming, but he answered. "He said he's hungry and asked for his mother."

Anna turned back to the boy. "Thank you, Snkt. We will get you something to eat in a moment, when we're finished."

Mostafa didn't translate her words that time, but Anna ignored it and spoke to Donny. "Hello. Are you five as well?"

"Yes," he said.

Anna didn't like his tone. She prodded, "And your name is Donny, correct?"

"Yes."

"Donny, do you know what year it is?"

"No."

"What is your full name?"

"I don't like my full name."

"I understand, but I want to get you back to your mommy. So, please, what is your name?"

"Mommy? I hate that bitch!" he yelled. His anger made everyone jump.

Linda's eyes went wide. "Oh my god." She staggered to her feet and paced the room, staring at Donny. Donny watched her, his sudden anger gone. His expression was devoid of any emotion.

It scared Anna. "Let's move on. Lorenzo, are you five years old?"

"Yes, ma'am, and I know my whole name. Do you want to hear it?"

Anna smiled and nodded.

"My mom named me after my daddy, Lorenzo Paldera the Second. Do you like it?"

Anna could see Lorenzo needed reassurance. She was about to tell him he had done well, but Ian moved forward with lightning speed. He picked Lorenzo up by his hair and threw him against the wall as if he were trying to kill him. Mr. Green and Mostafa rushed to stop him.

Linda ran to the kitchen and returned with a heavy metal bowl. She knocked Ian over the head with it, stopping everything.

Lorenzo was huddled in a ball on the floor. Snkt just stood there and watched, but Donny dashed over to Lorenzo. Anna thought he was going to help Lorenzo, but instead, he kicked him and hollered, "Get up, you little bitch. Stop crying. Fucking little bitch!"

Anna hurried forward and pulled Donny away. She helped Lorenzo up, then tried to shepherd them both to the kitchen. Donny resisted. Since Ian was breathing heavily, glaring at Lorenzo with hatred in his eyes, Anna turned to Mr. Green for support. He took Donny's arm and guided him out of the room. Snkt scurried after them.

The remainders of Mostafa's half-eaten feast were still on the counter. Anna told the boys not to speak to each other, then made sandwiches and served them on three plates. Mr. Green left, which made her nervous. Even though the boys were only five years old, they scared the living shit out of her. She didn't want to have to break up another fight. Donny was crazy, and Linda's reaction indicated he must have been terrifying. Lorenzo had to be equally as bad based on what Ian had done. To top it off, she couldn't believe she was serving Snkt Khet lunch.

She heard the conversation resume in the community room but decided to ignore it. She needed to collect her thoughts. An idea came to her. It was going to be a hard sell for everyone, but she had to try to save the boys' lives.

She figured it might be a mistake to leave Lorenzo and Donny together, so she sent Donny to eat in their room and told the others to stay in the kitchen.

When she walked back into the common room, Mostafa was speaking angrily. "It seems Anna and Mr. Green have not been affected by any of these devils. They do not get a vote."

"That's where you're wrong," Linda said. "Since they're the only two who have nothing in common with the monsters, they will have to be the deciding factors."

Anna coughed to get their attention. "Can someone bring me up to speed?" she asked.

Everyone looked at her, but it was Mr. Green who answered. "Well, we are in a quandary. You know what this Khet kid did. He killed millions of heathens to save the world from a false religion—"

Mostafa cut him off. "Do not justify the heinous actions of a deranged person. He slaughtered children and women."

"Look here," Mr. Green said. "I understand, and I know what your choice will be. Let me finish." He waited to make sure Mostafa stayed silent. "Like I was saying, Khet killed a lot of people. And it seems Donny, or Donald Walters, um, he…"

Mr. Green couldn't get the words out of his mouth, so Linda took over. "Anna, do you remember his name? Donald Walters? The Donald Walters who kidnapped twenty little girls and raped and murdered half of them." Tears formed in her eyes, and when she went on, her voice shook. "The Donald Walters who killed his mother and decapitated her. The Donald…" She broke into sobs. After a moment, she composed herself. "The media called us the Strong Eight. Because we fought back and escaped."

Anna was crushed to learn Linda was one of the survivors. "Linda, I'm sorry. I didn't know."

Linda's face contorted with pure hatred. "I watched as they electrocuted that fucker. And the gods, or whoever, are telling me I have to go through that again or let Khet go free?"

No one else spoke, so Mr. Green took control of the conversation. "The Lorenzo boy, well, he's easy. Based on what you said, it seems he did God's work by killing many abominations."

Ian sprang up and punched Mr. Green in the nose and stomach. Anna tried to stop him—she begged for someone to help her—but they just sat there. Ian hit Mr. Green until he was tired.

When Ian stopped, sucking in air and trying to catch his breath, Anna yelled, "What is wrong with you?"

"I told that ignorant piece of crap what would happen if he said one more injustice."

Mr. Green, still on the floor, laughed and spat blood out of his mouth. "I never thought a man like you would get the better of me. If I were home, I would have tanned your hide."

Anna shook her head. She had to sit down because everything was too much to bear. "Ian, please explain what Lorenzo did."

Ian rolled his neck and said, "Lorenzo Paldera is a terrorist. A mass murderer. In my time, he's on the run. So far, he's killed over ten thousand people. He targets individuals in my community."

"And what community is that?" Anna asked.

"The One Union!" he yelled. "He targets the One Union."

Anna didn't recognize the name and was afraid to ask. She looked to Linda for help but got nothing. "Ian, I'm sorry," Anna said, "but what is the One Union?"

Mr. Green started laughing uncontrollably. He answered her through his gritty smile. "He's an abomination. A man who goes against God and lies with other men."

When Anna understood, she hid her face, disgusted by Mr. Green's behavior. Everyone sat in silence. They all seemed lost in their pasts except Mr. Green, who looked to not have a care in the world.

Anna wanted them to take her seriously, so she made sure her thoughts were composed before she voiced them. "Okay, so the boys in there grow up to be a rapist and murderers. But right now, they're so young. Maybe we can teach them to be good and reshape their minds. That way, we're not killing innocent children. Because at this moment, they are innocent. They haven't committed any crimes."

Mostafa shook his head. "You would take that chance? It's a foolish dream to think you can change such a man as Snkt Khet."

"Or those sodomites," Mr. Green said. "They won't change either."

Ian and Linda started yelling at him. Anna could only understand a few disjointed words. Then a new voice cut them off.

"Occam's razor."

They turned in the direction of the voice. The Black woman had emerged from her room. She had short hair with small curls, and her gaze held a hint of authority. One of her eyes was lazy, as if she were tired.

She walked closer to them. "Occam's razor is the theory that the simple answer is usually the correct one. Even if that answer seems unlikely."

Mr. Green laughed. "Well, the lazy nigger finally decided to join us?"

She turned to him, wearing an expression of disdain. Mr. Green surprised Anna by looking unnerved rather than angry.

"And who are you?" Linda asked.

The woman didn't answer. She joined them and sat next to Mr. Green. Anna couldn't believe it when he didn't get up. He only stared at her, motionless.

The woman said, "We have White, Asian, and Muslim men. Hispanic, White, and Black women. We are all from different times. We are different in every way, from race to religion to sexuality to ideology. We represent the gray. The gray represents no color. It represents us." She gestured at Anna. "Why would you try to save all the boys when the rules state to choose one?"

Anna didn't know what to say. She felt as if the woman were reprimanding her like her husband did, but she was the only one who had provided a solution to their situation, and she wanted to defend herself. "Because it's a horrible decision to make. Why wouldn't we try?"

The woman shook her head. "I sat there for the past hour listening to you all arguing, but none of you are asking the right questions. It's a shame."

Linda stood and put her hands on her hips. "Now, you wait just a damn minute. Don't come in here all high and mighty after sitting on your ass while we try to figure this out. If you have the answers, then please share."

The woman laughed. "High and mighty, no. Tired, yes. This is my second time to come upon the Gray House." She waited for someone to respond to her news, but no one did. "Look, you all have been gifted a huge responsibility. You have the opportunity to take the information you gained here and reshape our world, reshape history. To save lives."

Mr. Green came to life. "You mean I can warn America of what's to come?"

That was a frightening notion to Anna. No one should have that much power—not her, and definitely not Mr. Green.

"Cure, if that were true, wouldn't we have heard or read about this?" Ian asked. "I know I haven't."

The Black woman smiled and nodded in approval. "Now you're asking the right questions. You haven't heard about it because you

18

can't tell anyone about the Gray House. I can't explain it. Just believe me when I say you won't be able to get the words out of your mouth."

Anna asked, "What do you mean we'll have the opportunity to reshape the world?"

"Well, first, you'll have to live with the choice you all make. Which evil will you let out? Which deaths will be on your hands? Second, you can become positive advocates, assist victims, or help shape new laws." She glanced over at Mostafa.

"Very interesting," he said. "But I'm curious. What decision did you have to live with?"

The Black woman bowed her head and spoke without looking at anyone. "I've been waiting over ten years for this day since I learned I would be the one to come back as the Explainer. I haven't looked forward to it."

Anna tried to ask the woman what she meant, but Mostafa put his hand up. "Please, Anna, let her answer my question."

The woman met Mostafa's gaze and set her shoulders straight. "The first time I arrived, it was May of 1968, and my world had been crushed. A great African American civil rights activist, a man who fought for equality, had been killed a month prior, and guess what little boy was here in my grasp? His murderer. I was elated to know I could erase that child and change what had just happened. But I had to stop and listen to my fellow members' arguments about the other two children."

Anna's heart stopped in its tracks. When she realized the choice the woman had lived with, she was afraid to hear who the other two children were.

"Will someone tell me who this civil rights fellow is or was?" Mr. Green asked.

"No, we will not," Linda said. "Ma'am, can you please continue?"

The woman eyed Mr. Green but said, "The second child was Pope Roberto Leon. He killed over four hundred thousand people in 1750. The third was Khopesh Khet. In his time, he killed thirty-six million people. How could I win with saving just one man?"

"I've never heard of Khopesh Khet," Mostafa said.

19

"Of course you haven't. He was Snkt Khet's brother, but now, if you do your research on him, you'll see he died in childbirth because we chose to let the other live." She took a breath. When she continued, her voice was hard. "I had to make an awful choice, to let that monster go free, and when I came back to my time, there was another Khet."

Mostafa put his head in his hands. "Well, then you made the right choice, because from what I've learned today, Snkt killed five or six million of my people. So you saved many lives."

They sat in silence.

Then Linda laughed. Everyone looked at her as if she had lost her mind. She said, "I know what you're all thinking. You're going to let the rapist go because only a handful of children died. Well, fuck all of you!"

Anna had to admit the choice sounded fair. They were there to save lives, and the math added up.

Everyone fell deep into thought again. After a while, Mr. Green broke the silence. "I'm not going to sit here and let little girls be violated. My vote is going with God. We need to let Lorenzo go."

Anna glanced at Ian. She felt sorry for him. She supported gay rights, and no one should die because of someone else's bigotry.

Ian rubbed the bridge of his nose before he spoke. "Mr. Green, I am trying to be patient with you because you're from a foul time. But keep it up, and you'll be spitting up a lung."

"Well, we have to vote, don't we?" Mr. Green asked. "I'm putting my vote in, and as a man, I'm giving you my reason. So you will have to live with it."

Ian stood up and yelled, "Did you know my husband died two years ago? We were going to start a family, but that murderer in there robbed me of that. He blew up a park that held a parade for my community. There were women and children there. My husband was there."

The Black woman stood and faced the others. "Listen, you all have a vote. Mr. Green says to let Lorenzo go. That's one down. I'll vote too, but I'm also here to be the Explainer. Which leads us to that. Before we vote on which child gets to live, you must vote on who has to come back to explain all this to the next participants of the Gray House."

"What if there's a tie?" Anna asked.

"Then the children will have to vote."

Anna thought that would be the worse option. The children were so young. Would they even be able to comprehend what they were being asked? She studied Mr. Green, remembering the small ways he'd changed over the last few hours. He was watching Ian, wearing the same confused, hesitant look as before—as if he didn't know what he believed.

"I vote for Mr. Green to come back," she said. Linda and Ian opened their mouths to speak, but Anna continued. "I know that sounds crazy, but I think this situation has altered his perspective a bit. He sees you as people now. Maybe he doesn't like things about you, but it's progress. And coming back would help him as well. He could continue to learn."

Linda gaped at her as if she'd lost her mind, but the Black woman said, "I agree with Anna. It could help him define a better future for himself and the people around him."

Linda looked outraged. "I would never give such power to a poor-minded man like him."

"Linda, maybe they're right," Ian said grudgingly. "He knows now that he has a negative impact on the growth of man but that the world evolves anyway. If he can change the way he thinks, he can help others do the same."

Mr. Green shook his head. "I want to thank you all for thinking of me, but I need to decline. I don't own land, so I'm not the person to be explaining anything."

Linda said, "Not owning land doesn't limit people the way it did in your time. I think they're right. As much as I don't want to admit it."

"It's not just that, ma'am," he said. "The future is frightening. I don't know about everything that happens as the rest of you do. I don't know how to change anyone's mind. I'm not the man for the job."

"But you changed *your* mind," Mostafa said. "And that is exactly why it should be you, my friend. Because of what you've learned here today, you may have more influence than you think."

Anna watched Mr. Green. She saw something shift in his eyes. "Well, all right. If that's what the group thinks."

Everyone looked at each other in agreement. Mr. Green would be the next Explainer.

It seemed too soon to vote on which boy to set free. Anna wasn't ready, so she said the first thing that came to mind. "Doesn't anyone care who's pulling these strings? How can we change time like this? Who's behind this?"

The Black woman said, "I don't know who brought us here or who controls this place. I've been to many libraries to research these questions and have come up blank. It's 1986 now in my time, and I've found nothing."

That got Anna thinking. "Did you ever run into the other people you met here?"

The Black woman smiled. "In a way, yes, but not in person. The people I was here with helped reshape my future. One gentleman spoke of this place in his poetry. You know him as Shakespeare." She laughed.

"You never told us your name," Linda said.

"And I never will. Now let's get down to the vote."

That surprised Anna. Why was the woman trying to be mysterious?

"So, Mr. Green," the woman said, "is your vote still to let Lorenzo the terrorist go?"

"Yes, ma'am."

"Okay." She turned to Mostafa. "What is your vote?"

"I wish I could convince you all," he said. "Snkt should not be freed. We don't truly know the circumstances that led to Khopesh Khet's reign, but I know firsthand what Snkt has done. He is a mass murderer, and because of him, I don't know where my wife and children are. Whatever your vote is, do not let him go free. If I am to save lives, I have to vote for Donny the rapist. He is the only choice that makes sense. I know it is cruel to let innocent girls be hurt, but the number of lives we save is the key."

"Thank you, Mostafa," the Black woman said. "Linda, what is your vote?"

Linda looked around at them. "I'm a survivor, and what happened to me shouldn't happen to anyone. To be raped as a child changes the way you view the world. You don't trust anyone, and you can't be touched. I've been through years of therapy, and if I can stop that from happening to me, I will. I'm sorry to say I'm going to vote with Mr. Green. I didn't choose to be raped, the Muslim people didn't choose to be born Muslim, but gay people choose their path. So I vote for Lorenzo as well. Ian, I'm sorry."

Ian nodded but didn't say a word.

"Okay," the Black woman said. "That's two votes to let Lorenzo the terrorist go and one vote for Donny the rapist. Ian, you're next."

Ian focused on Linda. "First, let me say that being gay is not a choice. I was born this way. I understand why you've all voted the way you have, but I hope to change some of your views. The rapist shouldn't be allowed out, because children don't deserve to be hurt. It's the duty of an adult to protect the innocent. I'm sorry, Mostafa, but Khet should be freed. I know five or six million people is a lot, but who's to say how many Lorenzo will kill? He's still on the loose. I vote for Snkt to be set free."

Before anyone else could speak, the Black woman shook her head. "I was going to cast my vote last, as the Explainer should, but I have to state my view now. This is my second time here. I sacrificed my self-worth and let a man who fought for the rights of his people die." She looked at Mostafa. "I tried to save the Muslim community, only to come back to my time and see that I couldn't save them all. I know you haven't lived that reality, but I have, and I want my last vote to mean something. Because of that, I'm casting my vote for Khet as well. I will not sit by and let little girls be raped or gay people be killed because of who they are. So, with that said, that makes two for Lorenzo, a mass murderer of the gay community, one vote for the rapist of little girls, and two for Snkt to be freed. Anna, it falls to you. And remember, if you make a tie, the vote goes to the devils in the other room."

All eyes were on Anna. "I need time," was all she could say.

She went back to the room she shared with Mostafa, lay on the cot, and thought through everyone's speeches. She knew they all believed their views were the best option, but she had to make the final decision. There was a lot to think about. What was the lesser evil? It was easy to say the rapist should live because it would save lives, but it was hard since she knew one of the survivors. But how could she let millions of people die at the hands of Khet, or tens of thousands because they were gay? It would be the greatest decision she ever had to make, and it was worse knowing she would have to live with her choice. Would she be ashamed of herself like the Explainer was?

She took over an hour to decide and make sure she understood her decision.

As she shuffled into the circular gray room, all eyes were on her. "Thank you for waiting," she said. "I know you all want to go home. I've considered each of your views. Ian, I agree with you that people are born gay. It's not a choice, and it's unfair for your people to be murdered because of it. But I'm not from your time. I don't know the implication of what's happening. Linda, you're correct as well. No child should be raped or hurt. I'm a mother myself, and if someone hurt one of my children, I would go to the ends of the world to right that wrong. But I also understand that your situation, as cruel as it is, is the lesser of two evils."

She took a breath and said, "Mostafa, the Khet family has wronged your people. Snkt slaughtered men, women, and children blindly without cause, just because they practiced religion. I have no words for the atrocities you have endured. But it sounds like they already tried to save your people, and the universe still had a plan. Who's to say another group in the Gray House didn't choose to kill someone in the Muslim community for something they did? That's just it, isn't it? We don't know because there are millions of scenarios that can take place.

"From what I've learned today, the world has to have evil in it, and we have the unfortunate responsibility of choosing which we send back out there. I know I will have to live with my decision, but I'll never question if I made the right one because there is no correct answer. They're all unthinkable. But I know now that when one Khet died, another popped up to do even worse things. We can't save those people, no matter how much we want to. For that reason, my vote is to let others have a happy life in the past and future." She looked at Linda, then Ian, thinking of the horrible things that would no longer happen to them. "I vote to let Khet go free."

* * *

Anna woke the next day in total confusion. She checked the time on her phone. It was 5:58 a.m., two minutes before her alarm would go off. Did she dream everything that had happened? There was only one way to know. She grabbed her phone and looked up Donald Walters. Nothing came up. She searched for Linda Hernandez, survivor of rape, but there was nothing. Her heart pounded a million beats per minute. Did she save the little girls? Did she save thousands of people in the future?

The sound of her alarm made her jump. Her husband turned and started to moan himself awake. To avoid bothering him, Anna got out of bed and went to the living room to use her computer. She had to find Linda and discover what had happened to her.

She searched other keywords and looked through various social media sites, anything that would put her in touch with Linda. Just when she'd run out of options and was feeling discouraged, her phone rang.

It was from an unknown number. She answered. "Hello?"

"Anna, is that you?"

"Yes. Is this Linda?"

"Anna! Oh, Anna."

Anna listened to Linda cry on the other end. Finally, Linda said, "Listen, don't say anything on the phone. We need to meet. I'll text you an address. Can you come?"

"Of course."

Later that day, Anna pulled up to the address Linda had sent her. It was an old building with no name on the outside. She walked through the double glass doors and greeted Linda with a hug.

When Linda released her, Anna said, "I'm so glad to see you. I thought maybe it was a dream. I looked you up. Are you not the president of your company anymore?" It was another thing Anna hadn't found during her search. She'd felt bad about it all day. Was it because of their decision?

Linda gave a soft laugh. "No, I'm not. But don't worry about that. Besides, there's someone here I want you to meet."

Anna followed her along a corridor and down an elevator, then through another hallway. She felt butterflies in the bottom of her stomach and second-guessed if she should have come. What if Linda tried to hurt her?

"Linda, where are we going?" she asked. "And who are we going to meet?"

Before she could get an answer, they came upon a door marked G.R.E.R.S. It was the company Anna had applied for, the one that had rejected her. What was going on?

When they went through the door, the Black woman from the Gray House greeted them. "Good morning, ladies," she said. "Anna, let me introduce myself. Sherrie Whitehead, CEO of G.R.E.R.S., or Gender, Race, Religion, and Sexuality Council of the World."

Anna was still in shock. She turned to Linda and asked, "You work here? But when we voted, you said gay people choose their path. You voted to free Lorenzo."

Linda smiled sadly. "I knew the others wouldn't, and I had to make sure the choice came down to you. Think of it as a test. A job interview."

Anna didn't know what to say. She didn't understand. Were Linda and Sherrie the ones who had taken her to the Gray House? Were Mostafa, Ian, and Mr. Green even real? She wanted to ask but only managed to get a few murmurs out.

Sherrie smiled and said, "Let me be the first to welcome you to your new job. That is, if you accept?"

The End

Friday, July 7, 2017 – 7:00 p.m.

The room had a thick odor about it, like a mixture of stalled beer and old cotton. It reminded Nate of when he was a child and had to go to his grandparents' house so his mother could go to her night job. He'd hated that she hadn't understood he was old enough to be home alone. That he could take care of himself.

He hated that he had to come to the stupid support meetings, too. He hated everything about the place. The walls were long overdue for a paint job, yellowed where they used to be white, and the air conditioner wasn't quite blowing cold air. It was like he was in a car in summer with the windows rolled down. He kept questioning why he even bothered to come. He couldn't stand listening to those pathetic excuses for men blabbering about how depressed they were.

Tina's voice brought him back to reality. "Nate, would you like to speak tonight?"

Nate ducked his head and thought, *Oh god.* Why was that woman constantly up his ass to talk? She knew he didn't want to share. She fucking knew. He thought maybe she wanted to fuck him. Maybe she wanted to wrap her small lips around his dick and hum the national anthem. She would be the sort of sicko who preyed on a weak person.

His wife's best friend was named Tina too, but he hadn't seen her in a long time.

He pushed the thought away and let his mind take him to even darker places. He fantasized about taking Support Group Tina in the back office and jamming his dick up her dry ass. He could picture it; he would bend her over her desk and tell her to shut up because he couldn't stand the sound of her voice. He imagined her trying to pull away, but he would make her take it.

"No," was all he said.

"Okay. Well, let's move on. George, are you ready to share?"

"Yes, I am. Thank you." George, a balding older man, shifted in his chair and almost fell out of it. "Sorry. I'm just nervous. Hello, everyone. My name is George, and I lost my wife two months ago."

"Hello, George," everyone said in unison.

George continued. "I haven't been able to sleep at night. I know I'm supposed to pick up my usual routine, but I used to take care of Linda at night, and now the thought of lying there…"

He started to sob. Nate watched, disgusted, as Tina the facilitator got up and hugged George. What kind of man cried like a fucking baby? People died every day. Life moved on.

Nate couldn't stand being there. He tuned out so he wouldn't have to listen to all the talking and crying. His mind drifted to the night of his first date with his wife. He'd been so nervous. It was supposed to be a blind date, but he'd found her Facebook page and stalked her profile. He wouldn't say he fell in love, but he'd liked that she was a party girl. She had posts of her going out with friends, pictures of her posing with some shots. His favorite was a post she'd written about one-night stands. He hadn't been able to decide if he should jack off beforehand and play it cool on the date or go in strong and hard and try to get her wet. He'd known she was going to be fun, and his dick had swelled every time he thought about how the evening was going to go. But he was glad he decided to play it cool because they talked the entire night about everything. He even bought her a present.

Tina's shrill voice brought him out of his thoughts again. "Well, that's it for tonight, gentlemen, but you have homework for next week." She stood and fumbled to close her folding chair.

"Rule number one," Henry said, "is do not talk about Fight Club."

Some of the men in the room laughed. Tina rolled her eyes and said, "Ha ha, Henry. I take it you've been waiting to say that for a while?"

"You caught me, boss lady," Henry said, a broad grin on his face.

Henry was around Nate's age and second-in-command at the meetings. Where Tina kept order, Henry tried to make the situation light—as if losing a loved one could be easy. Their tag team routine didn't impress Nate. He saw right through their act of trust and support and hated the thought of opening up to them.

"I'm glad we can joke and laugh," Tina said. "That's a good sign. Your homework is to write your wife a letter. Tell her whatever you want to say. You'll bring it next week and read it out loud as part of your therapy."

Nate was appalled at the idea. He didn't want to think about his wife, let alone write to her. He wouldn't participate. He only had to do two more sessions, and his obligation would be complete. Then he could go back to work and pretend the last few years hadn't existed. That he'd never met her.

The group started to create their circle of trust. That was the worst part of the meetings, and Nate's cue to leave. He quickly folded up his chair and placed it against the wall. He was almost to the door to the parking lot when they started chanting.

"We are never alone."

He pushed through the door and let it close behind him, cutting off their voices. It opened again almost immediately. Henry followed him out. "Nate, can I take a few minutes of your time?"

Nate didn't want to linger. The last time he'd stayed, he'd been cornered by George giving him the business card of an escort service to call if he got lonely.

But he said, "Sure. What's up?"

"I know you've been attending for a few days now, and I want to know how you're doing with finding a sponsor."

"Sponsor?" Annoyance and disgust welled up in Nate. "Look, dude, thank you, but no thank you. I don't need support or a shoulder to cry on. I need to get back to my life. So, no offense, but fuck off."

Before Henry responded, he repositioned his feet, as if getting ready to protect himself from Nate. Then he said, "Anger."

Nate squinted and asked in a dry tone, "I'm sorry, but what are you blabbering about?"

"Nate, there are five stages of grief. You are in the second stage. Anger. And I want you to know I went through it as well. I didn't want anyone feeling sorry for me like I was some reject. But I'm here to help with your transition."

Nate threw his hands up. "Hey, man. Like I said, I don't want to hear your story. Go find some other sap and sell it to him."

He turned and walked to his car. The night was warmer than usual. A bead of sweat stung his eye. As he wiped it away, he noticed the wind had picked up. The palm trees swayed, their fronds dancing to a beat he couldn't hear, telling him to just go with the flow.

He could hear Henry's footsteps behind him. "Nate, just listen to me for a moment. I don't want to sell you anything but friendship. At least take my phone number, and when you're ready to talk, call me, and we can go for a drink. How does that sound?"

Nate stopped but didn't turn around. He couldn't take his eyes off the trees. They reminded him of his wife. Of the time she got Lasik surgery and saw the green leaves of a palm tree for the first time without her glasses. It was as if she had never seen a tree before. She explained to him how the lines of the leaf were a sharp yellow she had never seen. That was one of the best days of their marriage. All she'd wanted to do was stop and look at normal things people missed while being caught up in the rat race of life.

Since the trees brought him a good memory, he decided they were a message to stop and listen. "Okay," he said. "I'm not promising I'll call, but I will take your number. And you're wrong. I'm not angry. I'm furious."

On the ride home, he stewed in a mixture of sadness, regret, and self-pity. Everything reminded him of her, and all he wanted to do was forget. The quicker he could forget, the easier it would be to move on, but it didn't seem possible. He saw her in everything. He didn't even want to move on, but he didn't want to keep thinking about her either—about their argument and that she was gone and there was nothing he could do to bring her back.

When he pulled into his driveway, he sat there instead of going inside. His mind was so agitated he couldn't remember how he'd driven home. What route had he taken? He'd heard of muscle memory, but did that take over in times of need? As much as he hated it, maybe he did need to talk to someone about his feelings.

Later that night, Nate lay in bed, unable to fall asleep. He couldn't stop thinking about her, and it was affecting him in so many small ways. Like in the mornings when he'd make himself a cup of coffee and get her a glass of water. He wouldn't realize what he was doing until he made it to the room and she wasn't there. His muscles and mind had known what to do. He'd always made his coffee in the morning, and he'd always gotten her a glass of water.

He'd woken her up the same way every day. He would put his mug of coffee on his nightstand, away from her because she couldn't stand the smell of what she called his Black Death. He'd place the water on her nightstand, open her drawer, and get her a women's multivitamin, an iron pill, and a stool softener. He would then get the lotion out and start by rubbing her feet. She would wiggle from the cold breeze on her feet without covers, then moan at his touch. He would slowly move up her legs, and she'd turn over with a smile. She had the most beautiful smile that melted his heart every time he saw it. The shape of her lips and the way she looked at him said a million things. They told him she was happy and that she was open to him. Then they would make love.

He felt his blood pulsate and his dick get hard at the thought of her hands touching him. It frustrated him because he was tired of jacking off. He wanted to feel the warmth of a pussy. He wanted to hear the sounds it made, like a crisp soda being opened, as he pulled in and out. It drove him crazy, knowing it was him who made it slick, like ice did to tires on the road.

Irritated, Nate picked up his phone and the business card George had given him at his first meeting. He'd laughed when he'd seen what it was, but it seemed the laugh was on him. At the time, he hadn't thought he would use it, but the idea of being alone upset him. He dialed the number.

"Hello. Jessica Sucker speaking."

"Ah, yes. My name is Nate, and I'd like to use your services tonight."

"Well, of course you would, daddy. Your phone number is not coming up in my system. Will this be your first time?"

"Yes."

"Oh, daddy, we love taking virginities here."

"Oh, no. Not my *first* time."

Laughter. "Well, of course not. Tell me, daddy, did you choose someone on our website, or would you like to tell me what you're looking for?"

"Website?" Fuck, what was that? Choose a woman to fuck on a website? "Never mind. I'll try this another time."

He hung up and got his laptop. After he pulled up the company's website, he scrolled through the selection, astounded there were so many women willing to sell themselves for money. What was the world coming to?

Finding someone was too difficult. As he went through each page, he realized he was looking for her. A few were close matches, but then their mouths would be too small or their eyes too far apart. Nate was so overwhelmed he slammed his laptop shut. Then he broke down and finally cried.

Saturday, July 8, 2017 – 9:00 a.m.

Nate decided to complete the list of chores she had written for him to do. He looked at the first one and snickered. He should have taken care of it a long time ago. Lana would remind him every day about fixing stuff around the house, and when he hadn't gotten to it, she'd tacked it to the wall so he'd see it as soon as he walked in. He rubbed his fingers across each letter, knowing her hands had once touched the paper.

His chores didn't take as long as he assumed they would. Once he finished, he wanted to stay busy. He couldn't stand having nothing to do. Every time he tried to relax, he thought of her, and he didn't want to. But when he realized he wouldn't be able to stop, he decided to do his homework and write her a letter.

Lana, my love,

I'm writing you this letter to say how sorry I am. I miss you, and I'm sorry I made you cry. I'm an asshole. I freaked out. I can't believe the words that came out of my mouth. You shouldn't believe them either.

I can't wait to be with you again. I can't wait to be next to you and hold your hands. I can't wait to be with you, to kiss your soft lips, to feel the warmth of you. You mean everything to me, and I thought I was going to lose you. Lose you to our baby. I've heard my buddies talk about how their wives love their children more than them, and for one selfish second, I didn't want to share you. Please forgive me. Of course I want a family with you. How could I not? I'm sorry. I didn't mean it.

I love you more than you can understand. I miss you even more. Please forgive me for that one stupid sentence. I take it back.

Your husband, your friend, your lover, and your indebted slave,
Nate

He sat there for a long time, staring at what he'd written. It felt odd to get it out, to tell her how sorry he was. He had said it so many times in his mind, and to finally see it in print meant something.

He decided he would take it to the support group and read it out loud. That way, everyone would know what an asshole he was. Everyone would know what his last words to his wife were. They would know their support group could never help him wash away his sins. And afterward, he'd hide the letter in her journal so it would be with her, in a way. He remembered buying her the journal, a softcover one with a picture of lilies on the front, and how she would write in it for hours.

After showering and eating dinner, Nate felt his mind start to wander. He remembered Lana waking up in the middle of the night once. It had been hot and sticky due to a monsoon. At the time, he figured she must have been uncomfortable, but when his eyes adjusted to the darkness, he realized she was crying.

"Honey, what's wrong?"

"I had a nightmare, that's all. Go back to sleep."

The nightmares had been happening more often, but when Nate tried to pressure her into talking about them, she said it was no big deal. He hadn't paid too much attention then, but he wished he had.

That got him thinking about her journal again. He'd promised her he would never read it, but it was all he had of her. Would she be mad if he read it after she was gone? He went back and forth. On the one hand, he desperately wanted to be closer to her. On the other, it would have violated her trust.

He decided against it. But he still felt so alone, and he didn't want to feel that way anymore. Being alone meant his mind would wander, and his thoughts always landed on her. He didn't want to talk to Henry about his feelings, so he got his laptop and looked at the website again. Fucking someone would release some of his built-up stress.

The website was easy to use. It had drop-down menus where he could eliminate some of the women. He figured there would be about fifty in his area and was blown away when there were over two thousand. He must have missed some new fad when he was married. Was there some development where women didn't care about discretion anymore? All their information was right there for the world to see.

He started by eliminating Asian, Caucasian, and Hispanic. He'd always had a thing for Black women. He liked the way they asserted themselves, so proud of who they were. That filter eliminated over eighteen hundred women from the pool. Next, he wanted someone with big lips, large breasts, and curves for days. He was already imagining himself running his hands up and down her hips. He laughed out loud when the search took out only twenty more.

He noticed there was a drop-down with education levels, but did that matter? It was just for fucking, right? But what if he wanted to talk and express himself? When he clicked for the woman to at least have a bachelor's degree, there were sixty left for him to choose from.

He started to sweat and realized he was nervous. What was up with him? It wasn't like he was looking for a wife. But he began to question himself. Was it cheating? He knew the answer, but did he deserve to experience pleasure when his wife was gone? When it was his fault he'd lost her?

Sunday, July 9, 2017 – 9:00 a.m.

Nate woke with a headache and didn't understand why. He tried to think of what happened the night before and came up short, so he looked around and found an empty bottle of Jack Daniels next to him on Lana's pillow. His head throbbed, and his mind was hazy, but as he thought hard about it, he remembered getting upset with himself for not being able to decide on a woman and drinking himself to sleep.

"You're just as bad as the pussies at the support group," he muttered. "Get your shit together and be a man."

After he showered, he called the number again, ready to choose.

"Hello, daddy. I see you're calling back. Have you decided who you'd like to pass the time with?"

"Yes, I have, darling." He tried to sound cocky since the last time he called, he'd sounded like a pussy. "But Big Daddy didn't see a cost on the website. How long will half a day set me back?"

"Well, daddy, that all depends on who you choose. What's her category number?"

"Three three two eight four." He went with her because he liked her smile and her eyes. Her eyes were sad. They called to him, asking him to take care of her. But her smile said something else— that she was cunning and devilish and liked to have a good time. He needed her badly.

"Let's see who we have. Three three two eight four. Ooh, lover, she is sexy, isn't she? What would you like her name to be for the day? Or do you prefer mystery?"

That wasn't a hard decision for him. "Mystery."

She laughed. "Very good. Let me get some of your information so we can get started."

Nate gave her everything she asked for, including his address.

"Thank you, Nate. She'll be there in an hour. And we have a special for virg... I mean, first timers. That means she'll stay the entire day and relieve you of any, shall I say, frustrations you have."

Nate was so excited he didn't realize they hadn't talked about the price until she hung up. He had five thousand dollars in the house and figured that should be enough.

He went to his bar and saw it wasn't stocked for a woman. Lana wasn't a big drinker, so all he had was some margarita mix. He ran to the store and purchased wine, crackers, Jack Daniels, cheese, and grapes.

When he got home, he showered again, then sat in his living room and looked around. There were pictures of him and his wife everywhere. Should he take them down?

The sound of the doorbell answered his question. It was too late. She was already there.

"You got this, Nate," he muttered. "Get your ass up and take control of your life." There he went talking to himself again.

When he opened the door, he was amazed. She looked better in person than she did on the website.

"Hello, Nate. I'm Lily," she said in a Southern accent.

She didn't even wait for him to invite her in. She pushed herself against him and slid into the house. Nate couldn't take his eyes off her. She had on a hot-red miniskirt with a see-through lace black shirt. She didn't have shoes on, and her hair was in some kind of messy high bun.

Lily sauntered around the house and found the wine and Jack. "Jack on the rocks kind of man, huh?" she purred. "How about I pour us some drinks?"

"I got a mixture of things for you, but yes, Jack is cool." He was still trying to figure out if he should be sitting or standing. He didn't want to look like an idiot.

"Relax," she said. "You don't have to be tense with me. I'm here to help you. Stop standing there like a dope and sit down. I'll make us some drinks, and we'll see where the day takes us."

That was what he needed. He liked that she was going to take care of him. His dick was throbbing from blue balls, and he was having trouble concentrating. He decided to start some small talk to help ease his nerves.

"Lily. Is that short for Lilith?"

She continued to pour the drinks and said, without looking at him, "Nate. Is that short for Nathaniel?"

He didn't like her response. "Very cute. Aren't you supposed to be making me feel better or something? I'm trying to come up with small talk here, and you're making it hard."

Lily walked over to Nate and handed him a drink. She took a sip from hers and bent down to face him. Her eyes never left his. As she put her glass on the floor, he could see that she had a piece of ice between her lips. She spread her legs and sat on his lap.

"What is it you desire the most?" When she whispered in his ear, the ice made her breath feel like a cool breeze.

That drove him insane. He desired so much that he didn't know how to answer. As he weighed a response, Lily started to move her hips from side to side. The pressure hurt and felt good at the same time. He grabbed her ass and made her press down harder, then started rocking with her.

She laughed. "What is it you want, Nate?"

"To be inside your warm pussy."

Lily stood and pulled her skirt up, revealing that she was not wearing panties. She took her shirt off, and her generous breasts bounced out.

"Stand up and take your pants off, Nate."

An hour later, Nate was exhausted but pleased. He admired the pool of his cum on her dark skin. He couldn't remember the last time he'd seen so much.

Lying next to him, Lily peered around the room and cleaned herself off. She pointed at a picture. "What was her name?"

He didn't like that she wanted to talk about his wife. "What do you mean? Why would you ask what her name *was*? She could be out of town on business. What is this?"

Lily sat up and turned to face him. "Relax, lover. When I went into the kitchen to make our drinks, I saw a lot of labeled Tupperware and thought she must be out of town, but the cards on the television stand say sorry for your loss."

Nate felt foolish. He didn't like anyone in his personal business, but she hadn't meant any harm. "Sorry. I'm not myself. Her name is… was Elaine, but I called her Lana. I don't want to talk about her."

Lily stroked his face with gentle fingers. Nate didn't like her expression, as if she pitied him. She said, "Sometimes talking about it is exactly what's needed."

That pissed him off. "Wow, I just wanted to fuck and not feel like a prisoner in my own mind."

Lily's eyes seared into his. "I understand you miss her," she said. "But this is why I'm here, to help you. So let me. What is it that's holding you prisoner?"

Nate stood and put his pants on. He was having a hard time with the zipper, so he gave up and sat on the couch with his shirt in his hands. She was right. He was paying her to make him feel better. Why not talk about it?

He shrugged. "The last thing I said to her. The fact that I can't fix it. I can't take it back. I don't know how to move on from that."

Lily joined him on the couch and put her hand under his chin to make him look at her. "Honey, that's easy. You can't fix it, and you can't take it back. You have to move on from it because what's done is done. You have to know in your heart that your wife knows you didn't mean it. Couples say things in the heat of the moment all the time they wish they hadn't, and guess what? They still stay together because they know one another."

Nate sat there with his mouth open like an idiot. He could only hope she was right.

Monday, July 10, 2017 – 9:00 a.m.

When Nate woke up, he couldn't remember if he'd dreamed or not. It was the best sleep he'd had since losing his wife. Lily had taken care of him, and her presence was worth the cost. Then he realized he didn't even know how much it cost. He hazily recalled telling her where the money was and to get what she was owed. He was upset with himself. What had made him do that?

He opened the nightstand, counted what was left, and was shocked to see she'd taken four thousand dollars. Well, that was his own damn fault. Or was he drugged?

He couldn't think of what he wanted to do for the day. He knew Lily was right and he had to forgive himself, but he didn't know where to start. After a few minutes, he decided to read Lana's journal. He had to know what was bothering her at night. He wanted to feel closer to her and convinced himself reading her words would do that.

He rolled over and opened her drawer. Her journal was right where she'd left it. He smiled at the flowers printed on the front. Lana had hated real flowers. She never understood why other women liked to receive something that would die.

He held the book for several long minutes before opening it to the first page. It was blank, so he continued to flip through. To his astonishment, every page was blank. There wasn't a single word written in it, but he knew he'd seen her writing in it all the time. Hadn't he?

Nate rifled through her drawer to see if there was another journal. When he didn't find anything, he tore the house apart looking for one. Again, he found nothing. It didn't make sense. He'd never actually seen the pages, but he recalled her scribbling away and making him promise never to read it. Was it some sick joke she was playing on him to see if he would break his promise? All it did was piss him off because he couldn't even confront her about it.

Tuesday, July 11, 2017 – 9:00 a.m.
Nothing.

Wednesday, July 12, 2017 – 9:00 a.m.
Nothing.

Thursday, July 13, 2017 – 9:00 a.m.

"Hello, Henry speaking."

The last couple of days had been sheer loneliness for Nate. He'd been so sure that if he could be closer to Lana through her journal, it would help him escape his misery. But instead, he'd taken a nosedive into nothingness.

"Hey, Henry. It's Nate from the support group. Can we meet? I'm not doing so well."

"Of course. Let's get some breakfast and talk. We can meet at the FRP in an hour."

"FRP?" Nate asked.

"Yeah, the Final Resting Place restaurant at the crossroads of Sixth and Eighth. It's by the Bigs convenience store. They have good food. See you in a bit." Henry ended the call.

It seemed like a strange name for a restaurant, but Nate looked up the address and took off. As he pulled into the parking lot, he thought about the last few days and couldn't remember if he'd eaten. Just the thought of food had his stomach growling.

When he walked into the FRP, he saw a lot of biracial couples, and it made him wonder why he and Lana had never tried the place out.

"Nate, over here," Henry called from a table near the window. "Come on. Sit down." After Nate joined him, Henry asked, "What stage do you think you're in today?"

"Wow, man. No small talk for you, huh? Can we at least eat first?"

Henry smiled. "Sure."

Nate was agitated. He wanted to be there and talk to someone who had gone through the same thing, but he was also scared to expose himself. He hated feeling vulnerable.

They ordered their food and settled into an uneasy silence until their meals arrived. Halfway through eating, Nate blurted out, "Depression." He froze with his fork in one hand and his head down. After a moment, he looked at Henry. They stared at each other. Nate waited for Henry to say something supportive or encouraging, but Henry didn't say a damn thing.

"As a sponsor, aren't you supposed to comfort me or something?" Nate asked.

"No. I'm here to help you with the transition. Losing a loved one is difficult, and we all have to find our way."

"Find my way? Jesus, man. My wife is dead, and I can't tell her how sorry I am." He started dry heaving because he'd cried so much over the last few days that he didn't have any tears left. He tried to get himself together. He didn't need Henry and everyone else in the restaurant to see him like that.

"Nate," Henry said carefully, "tell me how your wife died."

Nate stood and threw his napkin onto the table. "Fuck you! How is dwelling on that supposed to help me transition or whatever the hell you're talking about? You can pay for the food."

He stormed out of the restaurant. Henry followed him without paying for the meal. "Nate, stop and think about what I'm asking you to do."

Nate couldn't get to his car fast enough. He wanted to punch Henry. Had the guy lost his mind?

"Why does it matter how she died?" Nate asked. "She's dead. Period."

He reached his car and fumbled with the keys. Before he could get in, Henry caught up and put his hand on Nate's shoulder. "Nate, listen to me. I'm trying to help you transition so you can move on. Try to tell me how your wife died."

Nate stood there and struggled to comprehend what Henry was asking. He thought back to the day it happened. He was sitting on the living room couch, upset his team had just lost the playoffs.

Lana burst into the room, excited, holding a white stick in her hand. "Baby, guess what?"

He wasn't in the mood to play the guessing game. He knew that any minute, his buddy Larry was going to start the gloating parade of his team winning another fucking year.

"We're going to have a baby!" Lana exclaimed. "We're going to be a family."

Nate couldn't figure out why she was so happy. He was furious. They were barely getting by, even with both of them working. He rarely got enough pussy due to their work schedules, and they were going to have some little brat in the middle of them, sucking all the life out of her?

"Oh, Lana, this isn't the best time for us to start a family. Maybe we should hold off and wait a few years. You know, until we're completely on our feet."

Nate didn't want to think about that wretched day. He pushed the memories away and said, "Henry, I can't. It's too painful." He slumped down to the pavement. He couldn't believe he'd thought Henry would help him feel better. Instead, he was pulling out the weakness in him.

"Nate, you're almost there. Just remember."

Nate relived how horrible he'd been. He pictured Lana's face turning from happiness to confusion. Confusion to sadness to anger. "What the fuck are you talking about?" she asked. "I can't believe you just said that."

He remembered that but struggled to summon up how she died. He tried to explain it to Henry. "I... I don't know. I can't remember."

"Okay, buddy, then what do you remember? Think."

Nate put his hands on each side of his face, practically pulling his hair out. "Lana stormed out of the house. I tried to call her, but she left her phone on the table. I remember writing her a letter."

Henry sat on the ground next to him. "You're doing great. Keep going."

Nate shook his head. "I don't know. I must have blacked out. No. Wait." He stared at nothing. Suddenly, his memories came flooding back.

Back to Friday, July 7, 2017

"Lana, honey, you have to eat something. Please?"

The only sound in the living room aside from Tina's pleas was the whir of the ceiling fan. Lana hated the noise it made. Fixing the fan was number one on the list of chores she had made for Nate. She'd been asking him to do it for months, and for the life of her, she couldn't understand how the noise hadn't bothered him. The sight of the list she'd pinned to the wall pushed her into another crying fit.

After two minutes of trying to get her breathing back to normal, Lana was able to muster a few words. "I'm nauseous right now. The last thing I want to do is eat. I know you're trying to help, but please just let me be for a while."

Tina nodded and walked into the kitchen. "I'm going to label the food and put it away. There's so much. I might have to throw some of it out."

Tina kept talking about the food people had brought, but Lana couldn't focus on her words. Instead, she watched the fan and listened to the thud it made every time it went around.

After a while, Tina came back into the room. "Honey, I think we've put the funeral arrangements off for too long. I've done as much as I can, but there are a few things we need to go over."

Lana had never planned a funeral. The thought of it put her on edge. It was supposed to be a good time in her life. She was going to be a mother. She should be daydreaming about baby names and nursery wall colors. Instead, the unknown loomed over her. She had to pick the last outfit Nate would ever wear, and the thought of choosing a coffin made her dizzy.

She didn't know what to do with her hands. All she wanted was to shield herself from the pain, but the unseen misery hovered all around her. "Tina, I can't. I don't want to. I know I'm supposed to be strong or something, but I'm not. I'm sorry you're planning everything, but I just can't."

That was all she was able to say for the remainder of the day. She was so confused and so angry with Nate. It pained her that she couldn't yell at him. Her mind kept returning to that day. She'd been so happy that it hadn't occurred to her to think of how Nate would feel. His anger over the baby had made her angry too, and she'd run out, leaving the house so fast she forgot her phone. At the time, she thought it was funny he couldn't call her. She'd driven around for a few hours, hoping that once she got back, he would apologize. Instead, the house was empty.

Saturday, July 8, 2017

Lana woke in a frenzy. For one fleeting moment, she couldn't remember where she was. The sight of her nightstand put her heart at ease. Her glass of water and pills were laid out for her like they always were. But in the back of her mind, she knew something was missing. She should be getting her morning massage. Where was Nate?

The memories came back, and her stomach constricted. Nate was gone. All she could do was curl up and cry.

Tina entered the room. "Oh, honey. I know it's hard. Just cry, sweetie. There's nothing I or anybody can say that's going to make it feel better. I brought you some yogurt and some water to help wash down your pills. I know you haven't been hungry, but please think of the baby."

Lana's face crinkled up, and the minute folds in her forehead crashed against each other. "How did you know what pills I take?"

"Did I get it wrong? I thought you told me Nate always brought you water in the morning to help you wash your vitamins down."

"Oh. I forgot I'd shared that. Hey, look, Tina, I'm sorry about yesterday. Everything is happening so fast—"

Tina sat on the edge of the bed. "Honey, you don't have to apologize. I can't begin to know what you're feeling, but I'm not going to let my best friend go through it alone. Besides, Nate would kill me if he thought I wasn't taking care of you."

They both laughed. Lana knew Tina was right. She reminisced about when Nate had gone out of town one weekend for work. He'd been worried sick she would be scared, alone in their new house.

Lana asked, "Remember when he called you, like, a thousand times to make sure you would stay with me that weekend?"

Tina nodded. "God, he was a mess. I always thought it was him who was afraid to be away from you. He kept saying you didn't like being alone. What rubbish."

Lana felt good lying there talking about Nate. Deep down, she knew he wouldn't want her sitting around feeling sorry for herself.

She ate her breakfast, took her pills, and lamented the fact that her morning sex routine was gone. As she made her way down the stairs, she grinned, thinking she could easily keep up a morning quickie. She thought of the first time she'd touched herself in front of Nate. The way his mouth fell open, gaping at her. The way his dick swelled as he watched her stroke her pussy and how it had taken all his strength not to come over and join her. He'd sat there and watched her almost orgasm. But in the end, he made sure he was the one to finish her off.

As she reached the last stair, Lana was startled by Tina asking, "What are you smiling at?"

Lana went to answer, but then she noticed the chore list she'd pinned to the wall was gone. All her good thoughts drained away. She pointed to the empty spot. "Where's the list I had right here?"

Tina tripped on her way to where Lana was standing. She shook her head and said, "I noticed how it upset you yesterday, so I took it down."

Tears came rushing down. "Do not touch our things!" Lana ran back upstairs, and the day was lost to despair.

* * *

Later that night, Tina appeared in the doorway, balancing a tray. "Lana, I have something that'll help ease you down a bit. And it's also a white flag from me. Can I come in?"

Lana looked up and saw that Tina had a white flag in an empty glass. She laughed weakly. "Come in, my old friend. I'm so sorry—"

"Oh, no, honey. Don't—"

"Stop cutting me off, Tina. Let me explain. That list was on the wall for Nate, and I just… just please don't move things right now, okay?"

Tina nodded.

Lana examined the tray. "Whatcha got there, anyway? You know I can't drink."

"Actually," Tina said with a sly grin on her face, "I talked to your doctor, and she said you could have a hot toddy. It's warm tea with a shot of good ol' Jack Daniels. You can have a maximum of two shots, and I can finish the rest. Besides, Nate wouldn't want this to go to waste."

They settled in and talked all night. Tina was true to her word. She finished the bottle, and they fell asleep with it between their pillows.

Sunday, July 9, 2017

Lana sat in a large, comfortable chair, waiting for George, the funeral director. Tina sat next to her, there to support her if she needed it.

The funeral home was exactly what Lana imagined it would be. Phony scriptures framed on the wall to help soothe loved ones, false hopes of being united again all over the room. The fake plants were comical. Nothing in that place was living. Even George seemed hollow.

He entered the room, carrying a large book. Lana's stomach did a turn. She'd saved that for the last selection. "Now, Elaine," he said, "I know this is overwhelming, but let me reassure you that I'm here to make this as easy as possible. Tina has selected everything but the casket. We'll stick to pages fifteen through twenty for your price range."

Lana skimmed each page. She didn't know why she had to pick one. Did Nate really care what color his coffin was? Did it really matter to him if it was airtight for fifty-plus years?

As she flipped through, one caught her eye. A small laugh caught in her throat. "This one will do just fine." The coffin was light brown with one flower on the lip to indicate it was closed. But when it was open, the flower was cut into two halves.

"Let's see," George said. "Oh, yes. Number three three two eight four, the Lily Flower. Very nice selection, my dear. Everything is now settled. I'll come back with the calculations."

Tina had stayed quiet for the most part, but she was clearly curious. "Why the laugh? And why did you pick that one? You hate flowers."

Lana reflected for a moment before answering. "You're right. I hate real flowers. On my first date with Nate, he brought me flowers, and I told him I wasn't impressed because they die. So he threw them away and bought me a flower that couldn't die. My journal has lilies printed all over it. He said they were there to remind me he would do anything to make me happy, and by writing in there, my thoughts would always be with him. He promised me he would never read what I wrote."

"Oh, that's beautiful. Do you still have the journal?"

Lana stood and paced the floor. She didn't know if she wanted to talk about her journal. It was private. "I hate this place," she said. "I hate everything it represents. These leeches prey on the weak and squeeze them for money to take care of a dead person."

Tina got up and hugged Lana. "I know you're angry, sweetie, and that's normal. I read a blog last night that said there are five stages of grief, and anger is one of them."

"How funny," Lana said. "I read the same article. But listen, I'm sorry. My emotions are everywhere right now. And to answer your question, yes, I still have the journal. I still write in it to clear my head. I've been having nightmares. Nightmares of darkness and loneliness. They're about Nate now, but they started when I got pregnant. Anxiety, I guess."

George walked in with the paperwork for Lana to sign. He started to go into the cost, telling Lana she could make payments, but she held her hand up. "Look, George, just get to the point. I have four thousand here in cash, so what's the balance?"

Later that day, the doorbell rang. When Lana answered, there was no one there, but on the doorstep sat a bottle of Jack Daniels, some cheese and crackers, and wine. She walked along her driveway and peered up and down the street, but there wasn't a car in sight.

Thursday, July 13, 2017

Lana showered and fixed her hair up. She was alone in her room, happy for the chance to get her mind in order. Nate's family had flown in on Tuesday, and she hadn't had any time for herself. Despite Nate's death, they all saw the silver lining Lana couldn't bring herself to be happy about: the baby. That was what everyone talked about, how Nate had left a part of himself there, but Lana didn't know how to feel about it. Nate hadn't wanted the baby.

She remembered that day so vividly. She had been in the bathroom, waiting for the longest single minute of her life. She'd hoped with all her soul the stick would read positive. All she could think was, *Please have a plus sign.*

Then it happened. Her heart fluttered. She couldn't believe it. There was a tiny person growing inside her, a part of her and a part of Nate.

She ran out of the bathroom and saw Nate glaring at the television.

"Baby, guess what?" she asked. When he didn't answer, she just yelled out through her excitement, "We're going to have a baby! We're going to be a family."

She saw the surprise on his face. Any minute, he was going to start jumping up and down, then run and hug her. He would bend down and stare at her belly and kiss their child growing inside her.

Instead, his expression turned angry. "Oh, Lana, this isn't the best time for us to start a family. Maybe we should hold off and wait a few years. You know, until we're completely on our feet."

She hadn't told anyone about their argument. She couldn't bring herself to say out loud that he hadn't wanted a family with her. That he'd left the house to get away from her and had died in a car accident. She couldn't even remember what she'd said to him. She just remembered needing to get out of there.

One thought had been running through her mind over and over again: maybe if she hadn't acted like a child but sat and talked it through with him, he would still be there. Or maybe if she hadn't tried to surprise him, he wouldn't have been so angry. All the little choices she'd made had led to his death, and she couldn't stop wondering what would have happened if she'd made different ones. She knew thinking about it wasn't going to help in the end, but she had no one to talk to about it. The one person she wanted to hold, to yell at, to cry with was gone.

Lana was brought out of her thoughts by a knock on her door. "Come in."

Tina opened the door and poked her head in. "Hey, love, are you ready? I gave you as much time as I could. The limo is outside, and everyone else is on their way to the church."

"Thank you for everything, Tina. I'll be down in a few minutes. I just need to get my notes."

Tina looked at her quizzically. "Notes?"

"Yes. I know it's not on the program, but I decided I want to talk about Nate today. A final goodbye."

Tina nodded and left the room. When Lana went to the nightstand to collect her things, she noticed her journal. She didn't know why, but she grabbed it along with the notes, hoping it would bring her courage. She had decided to tell everyone it was her fault Nate died, that they had gotten into an argument and that he'd left. She didn't deserve all the concern and kindness. They all needed to know she was cruel—that she'd been so fixated on her own wants and needs she hadn't considered Nate's feelings.

The ride to the funeral was quiet and uneventful. The driver didn't play any music or try to come up with small talk. Lana truly appreciated the small act of kindness.

She was the last to enter the church. Friends sat in the back, with family toward the front. The music was a slow, morbid dirge. As soon as she walked in, everyone stood as if she were getting married, as if it were nothing but a show she was putting on. All Lana could see was the casket.

She could hear someone crying like an idiot. As she sat down, she couldn't understand why so many people were around her, fanning her as if she were going to pass out. She wanted the stupid bitch who was screaming like a fool to stop. She looked up to see who it was and realized, to her humiliation, it was her. Tina was saying something to her, but through all her sobbing, Lana couldn't understand. The casket had set her off. She hadn't been expecting to see it. The flower said it all. It said, *I will never die. I will never open for you.* It said, *This is all your fault.* Her emotions were a mixture of hatred for herself, sadness for the baby, and pity for who she was about to become.

The pastor stood and said something Lana couldn't comprehend. Tina leaned in and made Lana focus on her. "Get it together, girl. You know Nate would want to kick my ass. Now, come on and show him it's okay for him to move on."

Lana closed her eyes, took a long, deep breath, and opened them. What she saw next was exquisite. It made her laugh. People looked at her as if she were crazy, but she didn't care.

There wasn't a real flower in the place. No bouquets flowing over the casket or carnations being passed out. Instead, there were thousands of paper flowers in all sorts of colors and shapes. Deep reds and purples, light greens and yellows, blues, browns, and golds. She loved it.

She leaned in and whispered to Tina, "Paper flowers?"

Tina smiled. "Nate would have wanted you to be happy, and real flowers would never do."

The choir had just finished with a beautiful selection when the pastor announced that Lana had a few words.

Tina squeezed her hand. "Love, you don't have to do this."

Lana shook her head. She knew everything was going to be okay. She went to the podium. As she set her notes in place, she noticed something sticking out of her journal and wondered if it was starting to tear apart.

She gazed out at the crowd and started with a small sob. "Hello, all." Tina stood and started to come toward her, but Lana said, "Sorry, I'm okay. No need to come up." After Tina sat back down, Lana continued. "You hear the words, that the loss of a loved one is hard but that in time, it will get better. But what you have to understand is they're just fucking words."

She heard the crowd gasp and realized she'd said the f-word. She didn't care. She just laughed it off. "I'm sorry, pastor. I'll make sure to throw in a bigger tip for today." Again, she heard murmurs. Tina sent her a thumbs-up for reassurance. "As I was saying, words are nothing but noise to fill the silence. But pain, that is real. There are no words to fill the hole in your heart. There are no words to fix the anguish you feel when you finally understand that death is absolute."

She looked at her notes. She was going to transition to how she didn't deserve their pity when she again saw the paper poking out of her journal. She pretended to shuffle her notes and opened the journal.

It was a folded piece of paper with her name written on it, and she instantly registered it as Nate's handwriting. She gasped and put her hand over her mouth, then opened the note and read. It began, *Lana, my love, I'm writing you this letter to say how sorry I am. I'm an idiot. I miss you, and I'm sorry I made you cry.*

Silent tears streamed down her cheeks. Tina rushed to her side, but Lana patted the air in front of her to indicate she was all right. The pastor gave her a glass of water and whispered that maybe she should sit down. But as Lana looked up at him, then at the crowd, she saw something even more amazing than the paper flowers.

Same day – Thursday, July 13, 2017

When Nate realized he had died, not Lana, his first instinct was to freak out. But Henry was there. Everything started to fall into place.

"Am I in purgatory?"

Henry put his hand on Nate's shoulder. "No, my friend. You're in the in-between. When a soul gets trapped here, it's our duty to help it transition. Most of the time, the lost soul has unfinished business. But your situation is a bit different."

Nate was listening, but he was also distracted by the elation of finding out Lana was alive. "What do you mean I'm a bit different?"

Henry gave a small laugh. "*You're* not different. Your situation is—when you don't realize you're dead. You can have a minor influence on the Live World, and that's not something we want. I'm here to help you realize it's time for you to transition."

Nate stared out at the horizon. "I don't understand. I know I died now, so why am I still here? I'm happy it's me and that Lana and the baby have a future."

Henry stood and extended his hand. Nate took it and was pulled to his feet.

"Nate, it was Lana who had your soul stuck here. That's what I meant by your situation. With the combination of you not understanding you died and Lana's sorrow holding you here, it makes an interesting shit bag, doesn't it?"

Hearing Lana's name sent Nate into a frenzy. "What does this have to do with her? What do I need to do for her?"

Henry started walking away. "All you have to do is listen."

That confused Nate, but he followed. "Henry, I have so many questions. What's next for me? Should I be on my knees praying for forgiveness, or is it too late? What would have happened if I hadn't called you—"

"Nate, slow down. That's not for me to discuss with you. My job is to help you move on. Understand?"

No, Nate did not understand. But he knew he wasn't going to get anything else out of Henry.

All of a sudden, Nate was no longer walking. He was in front of two large oak doors. "What the…"

Henry laughed. "Listen, in order for you to move on, Lana needs to let you go. Walk in and listen to her. That's all you have to do. She needs this just as much as you do."

Nate glanced at the doors and back at Henry, but Henry was gone. It was as if he was never there.

Nate opened the door, and there she was, in front of a church congregation. He walked in, and they locked eyes.

Same day – Thursday, July 13, 2017

Lana knew Nate couldn't really be there. But he was. He was there, looking at her with passion in his eyes. His body was a bit translucent. She couldn't quite see through him.

The crowd was starting to get restless, and she knew she had to say something. "I'm so sorry, everyone. Like I was saying, the pain a person feels when they lose someone is personal. That person has to go through the five stages of grief. Denial, anger, bargaining, depression, and acceptance. And believe me, in addition to being pregnant, I have experienced each one. Often, a person will transition between them, but I think I've gone through some at the same time."

The crowd laughed.

The rest of the speech was only for Nate. "Acceptance is the hardest transition to go through. As I said, loss is personal, and losing you was devastating for me. I was so excited to begin our family that I was engulfed in only myself. You didn't get the opportunity to celebrate with me. I'm so sorry. It's unfair that I will be able to witness all the life events our child will go through. It's unfair, but I know you are truly in a better place. My only ask is that you look after us from time to time. I accept you're somewhere I can't go, but I hope that one day, I will join you. So for now, my love, please accept that I love you more than there are stars in the sky."

Lana saw Nate smile and fade away.

The End

CIRCULATIONS

In the year 2027, a small company by the name of Orbit 12 sent its first manned rocket ship into space. Their mission was to settle on Mars. At a speed of thirty-six thousand miles per hour, they would reach their new home in thirty-nine days. The ship held twelve souls, with the oldest being the ripe age of fifty-six.

That man was Dlon Tung, a pioneer for the planet Earth. Before the Mars mission, he discovered the Hyperground, a faster form of travel that bankrupted airlines because the prices were a third of the cost of airfare. It was embedded deep underground and could travel at superspeed, meaning it could take a family of four from New York to California in two hours in perfect comfort. Dlon used that same technology to enhance space travel.

Dlon's Mars mission was supposed to be a one-way ticket, but the cosmos had another plan for humankind. Halfway through their journey, the crew discovered a wormhole in space. Not knowing where it would take them, they decided to alter their course to see if they could discover something beyond what they knew. What they found was another solar system, one with eleven habitable planets.

Dlon and his crew wanted to share their findings with Earth, but they worried humanity, which held tightly to its belief in God and religion, wasn't ready, so they returned to Earth and said the mission failed. Instead of telling the world what they discovered, they came up with a new world order they knew would take more than their lifetimes to bring about—a new way of life that valued science and knowledge. They poured billions of dollars into political campaigns, medical technology, and space travel.

Wars were fought to maintain the old way of life, and hundreds of thousands of people died by the day, but humanity's vision slowly turned away from religion.

Finally, their plan was in place. The campaigns to silence religion had worked. Dlon Tung had taken his vision of enriching the human race with equality and offered a new way of life—multiplanetary living. On Earth, which was renamed Planet One, he'd worked with the Council of the Human Race to create life-preserving organs, or LPOs, so life was no longer measured in time but in the enrichment of the human mind. As individuals gained knowledge, they earned the right to circulate, or move from one planet to the next, with the goal of reaching Planet Twelve and achieving enlightenment. Under the new way of life, there was no greater honor.

* * *

On Planet Two in the year 2127, a hundred years after the first circulation, Rachael sat in her room in complete silence. She kept going over the events of the day before, trying desperately to come up with an explanation, but her mind was numb. All she could do was stare at the gift her grandfather had given her.

It was supposed to be the day of her first circulation, her elevation to Planet Three. She had been so excited. Planet Two was okay, but it was only the foundation of the basic principles of life, and she wanted more. But her plan had been turned upside down when she'd learned of her inheritance. She'd never understood her grandfather's decision to revert to the old ways and allow himself to die, but he had assured her that when his life ended, he would give her the best gift—a way to guarantee she would be able to circulate. At the time, she'd assumed that meant he'd give her his DCs.

Digital Currencies, or DCs, had replaced paper money long before Rachael was born and were necessary for circulations. Everyone started their lives with the same amount of DCs, but each time they enriched their minds through knowledge, they earned more. When people accumulated enough and followed the natural progression, they would circulate, first from Planet Two to Planet Three, and so on. Without DCs, circulating was impossible.

But there was a way to get DCs without knowledge. and that was by inheriting them. That was rare because humankind was always in the pursuit of knowledge, with so many aspiring to make it to Planet Twelve. Rachael knew if her grandfather passed his DCs her way, she could be one of the elites who circulated early, at the age of twenty.

 Rachael's father had been furious when he found out about his father's decision to no longer use LPOs. It didn't make sense. Sir Benon had already circulated to eleven out of the twelve planets. Why would he give up all of a sudden? Not many people reverted to the old ways, and it was a true embarrassment for her family.

"It's a complete waste of resources for you to do this," her father had shouted as Sir Benon tried to explain.

"Son, men were not supposed to live more than one lifetime. We were not supposed to go against nature and stop the life cycle. We were supposed to pass knowledge down to our children to help the next generation become better than we were."

"Don't give me that bullshit! I gave up my first circulation to have a daughter. To teach her right from wrong. I'll be leaving her soon to circulate, and I know she will take the knowledge I have passed down. It's your duty as an Eleven to continue the journey. How could you do this?"

Sir Benon again tried to explain, but it seemed he was having trouble finding the words. That struck Rachael as odd because her grandfather was normally a loquacious man. He tried to touch his son's arm, but her father pulled it away and spat, "I don't want to hear this. You need to leave."

Rachael hadn't seen her grandfather again until the video was put in front of her the previous day. Even though she'd been forbidden to speak with him again while he lived, in her heart, she'd forgiven him. She didn't understand why he would want to die, but she was grateful to know she was his heir. Her grandfather was very important to her. He'd been a prestigious man on Planet Two, and it was a great honor for her family to have a high-ranking relative.

She'd only met him in person once, the day of his argument with his son, but throughout her life, she'd had many lessons from him on video. To see him in the flesh had been enormous for her.

But that day, all she could do was sit and look at her gift—a tall, dark hunk of junk. Why would Sir Benon do that to her? She remembered what he called it in the video: a grandfather clock. A relic from the old way. A machine to measure time.

Rachael watched the video again, trying to comprehend the motive for his betrayal.

"My dear granddaughter…" he began. He was in an all-white room that was otherwise empty. Rachael couldn't tell if he was in the center because she couldn't see any corners. It was as if he were in a bubble. He looked sad, and that seemed weird to her. After all, he'd made the decision to stop his journey. Hadn't he?

"As you are aware, I have traveled back to Planet One to live the rest of my life in solitude. I can only hope in my heart that you aren't as angry with me as your father is. You're very special to me, and my son made a great sacrifice to stay behind for you. As you know, deciding to have a child is special. In the old ways, it was the purpose of life. To fall in love and create a family was the means of living forever—passing your genes on to the next generation and witnessing the greatness or destruction they created."

Rachael had been a bit irritated the first time she watched the video and found she was getting a lesson. She'd wanted to understand his reason, but more than that, she'd been itching for him to tell her he was passing her his DCs.

"We strive to become great in the new way, but we are going about it all wrong," Sir Benon said in a lofty tone. "Dlon Tung states we have a duty to maintain the light of consciousness to make sure it continues in the future. He is absolutely right—it's just that the human race went about it incorrectly. The duty was to pass that light on, not keep it for ourselves. My dear Rachael, did you know it was I who requested your father and mother have you?"

That had been a complete shock to her. She knew her mother had circulated as soon as she could and that her father had stayed behind for her. She'd never taken her mother's actions personally, but she'd always wondered why.

Sir Benon went on. "Your parents did a great service for me and were rewarded well. They never asked why, but they knew you were important to me. I know you are awaiting my gift, and I know you will be quite upset with it. So let me get this part over with. I left all my DCs to my son as an extra thank you for staying behind with you."

Rachael's anger from the day before returned as if she were hearing his words for the first time. Her heart hammered in rage, and her mind forgot how to suck in oxygen and let it flow into her lungs. She was his heir, not her father! What better gift could he give her than his DCs?

"I can only imagine the look on your face right now or the thoughts going through your mind. My sweet, sweet girl, DCs are not everything. Dlon Tung is a great man, and I aspired every day to understand him. As you know from his Golden Rule, the only thing that makes sense is to strive for greater collective enlightenment. I believe I truly understand his words now. So I bestow upon you the greatest gift I could give. My grandfather clock."

A *ping, ping, ping* told Rachael she had received electronic mail. It read: *Hello, Rachael. Sir Benon left you a coded message we will be patching through in a few minutes. Thank you for letting TriCon serve you today.*

Rachael waited as Sir Benon's message came through. Once it was complete, she put on the decoder she and her grandfather had come up with. Her grandfather had a brilliant mind. He'd taught her all about coding and deciphering hidden messages. If an unwitting person had read the message, it would have appeared to have nothing to do with anything, but Rachael knew how to find the hidden meaning.

Her screen let her know it would take two clicks to decode, so she decided to go for a run. She was irritated the whole time. She'd thought she understood her grandfather, but everything was happening so fast she couldn't keep things straight. Plus, she hadn't been able to contact her father yet because he was still in transit to his next circulation. She wondered if he'd learned about his inheritance before he left. If he knew she was still stuck on Planet Two.

She made it through her front door just in time to hear another *ping, ping, ping*. She hurried to read the message. Her heart was beating extra fast, and not because of her run.

Hello, Rachael,

By now, you should have my grandfather clock with you at home. In the old ways, clocks were an instrument to measure, keep, and indicate time. You can see the clock has three words engraved on it. Research each word and use all the tools I taught you to determine the code to make the clock work. Once you enter the correct time into it, the bottom door will open, and the truth will be revealed to you.

But understanding the truth will come at a cost. I love you more than time itself, and you mean more to me than words can describe. I want you to go on your own journey to figure out for yourself what is the right path for you to take. You have the choice to continue with the new way and elevate at your own pace, or I present a new path for you—one that will explain my choice, and one only you can take. This choice is dangerous, but through it, you will discover the truth.

Well, that didn't answer anything. All the message did was create more questions. Why would her grandfather want her to find the answers to a new path? He had always guided her toward enlightenment. She wondered what had changed his vision so powerfully that he decided to revert to the old ways when he was so close to reaching Twelve. Not a lot of people made it. Many stayed between Planets Nine and Ten, where they found solace in understanding their true selves.

Rachael pulled out a piece of paper and wrote down everything she had discovered in the last two days. She'd found out her parents had her for Sir Benon and had been rewarded. That kind of answered her questions about her mother. She'd probably never wanted a child, so she had Rachael only to elevate herself. Rachael wondered if she would be able to do it too, to go through the special process of breeding another human being just to be elevated. She didn't want to think about what her decision would be.

Rachael also wrote that her father had given up elevating to stay behind and raise her. He'd made a huge sacrifice for her, and she would remember it for the rest of her life. All she could hope for was to one day be reunited with him to show how grateful she was for his love.

Next on her list was that her grandfather requested she be born, and she was created to be his heir. But why would he do that unless he'd already planned to end his life and go back to the old ways? She had so many questions, but she knew that had to be the point—she had to seek out the answers for herself.

Which led her to the final item on her list. The grandfather clock. She had been staring at it all day but hadn't looked closely enough to see any engravings. She would start there. Then she would research how to make the clock work to give herself a mission, a goal to move toward. She would go on the journey because Sir Benon had asked her to. She would put her trust in his hands.

Rachael stood in front of the massive machine and examined it. It was more than six feet tall and made of red cherry wood that shone as if it were freshly polished. It was actually quite beautiful. Whoever made it had put a lot of detail into it.

The clock had three doors with brass handles. The first door opened to the face, where the numbers were. Three arrows all faced the number twelve: one short, one medium, and one long. Rachael didn't understand what they meant, but she knew they must be part of entering the code.

She opened the glass door to study the gold-plated numbers more closely, then gently glided her fingers over the twelve. It was cold to the touch, and Rachael felt a shiver. Excitement coursed through her veins. She couldn't understand why, but she had a drive to make her grandfather proud of her. She had to get that thing to work.

Through the middle glass door, she could see a long golden rod with a circle connected to it. That didn't seem as interesting as the numbers. The rod just hung there. But when Rachael touched it, it moved from side to side, which made it more intriguing. She couldn't figure out what it was for but knew she would soon learn.

The last door was the largest and didn't have glass to see through. It was made of solid wood. Just as Sir Benon had said, there were three words etched into it. *Religion, Evolution, Enlightenment.* Rachael went to open the door, but it wouldn't budge. So, the secret was there, but she had to figure out how to get at it.

She made a plan. The easy part was the numbers. There were only twelve. The next step was to understand the three words and what role they played. Then she'd have to figure out how to make the clock work. She couldn't find an "on" switch. She tried voice command, but of course, that did nothing.

Her grandfather had said to use the tools he'd taught her. There was only one method she could think of; she would have to use numerology to solve it. The study of numbers was a crucial step in her mental evolution because numbers never lied. They were the truest form of fact and told a story of pure honesty.

Rachael thought back to her lessons with her grandfather. They were always something she'd looked forward to because they made her feel like she was one step closer to her circulation. Her lessons would start with a lecture and end with a reasoning session where she would have to take what she learned and apply it to a situation Sir Benon put before her.

The one that stood out most was her first lesson on numbers versus opinion. The lecture required a basic understanding of math, in which she was very advanced, and had talked about the meaning behind each number and how they represented everything. Rachael had been fascinated to learn that each number had a meaning. Sir Benon had turned the tables on her and asked who came up with numbers and their meanings. Whose opinion was it that made each number a fact? The better questions were what was a number, and how did it work in the universe? Rachael's task had been to determine if numbers were fact or an opinion of the human race. Those were the kinds of lessons she'd need to make use of, the thought processes she'd need to employ, to complete her grandfather's task.

Three weeks after receiving the clock, Rachael figured out the code to open the last door. But there was a lot to think about. She couldn't shake the idea that it might be a test. Her grandfather had indicated that if she entered the code into the clock, his truth would come to light, but what did that mean? What was the right path—her grandfather's new views or the Twelve and what they represented to the human race? The path that had ended wars and greed or what her grandfather had come to believe?

Rachael didn't know what to do or think. She decided to consult one of the Commanders of Truth in the Hall of Righteousness. Commanders were individuals who made it to Planet Eleven but decided they didn't need to move on. Surely, they had gained knowledge that might help her make her choice. She knew it would be a gamble. She had started on a path that took her away from the Twelve, and that wouldn't be received well. There was a possibility she could lose DCs. But she needed guidance, and the Hall would be the best place to get it. It was a massive center of intelligence: books from all over the worlds, gurus from all facets of life.

Rachael met with Commander Dean Le'gon, whom she knew had chosen not to continue his journey because he believed he was meant to teach. He'd returned to Planet Two to assist in the basics of evolution and help mold young minds. He also held a seat on the Council of Circulation, which determined when someone could circulate. Just having the right amount of DCs wasn't enough. People had to go through a trial with eleven commanders, each from a different planet, before being guided on their circulation.

It was eerie to talk to a commander, but Rachael told him everything. As she spoke, he sat in silence with his back straight and his hands in his lap.

When she finished, Commander Le'gon looked deep in thought. He studied her face before speaking. "Thank you for shedding light on this situation. I always wondered why a person with an elevation such as your grandfather's would decide to revert. I would like to ask you some questions before I make my judgment. The first is just a curiosity, so please bear with me. How did you come to find the code to open the door?"

Rachael was surprised he'd chosen that as his first question. She thought she would have to explain why she even started on the journey. But she went back into storytelling mode to explain her findings.

"Well, in understanding numbers, one needs to understand numerology, which is the branch of knowledge that deals with the occult significance of numbers. I also had to learn what each word etched into the clock had to do with each number. 'Religion' is defined as a particular system of faith or worship. 'Evolution' is the gradual development of something, especially from a simple to a more complex form. And 'enlightenment' is defined as an intellectual movement that emphasizes reason and individualism rather than tradition—the action of enlightening, or the state of being enlightened, which, of course, you already knew. So I had to look at each word and translate that into numbers.

"In numerology, one and two are the father and mother of the child, which is three. Three is well-rounded, balanced, and happy. It represents both the human and the divine. Its energy is that of the bringer of change." She blushed. "But I'm going off into a lesson, so please forgive me." She felt silly for saying so much. It had felt like one of her debates with her grandfather in which she had to present her findings.

She went on. "So, one represents unity, divinity, and wholeness. Four represents the human, the crossing of two lines constantly evolving. And five represents the enlightened human. Once I understood the meaning of each word, the code to enter was easy."

"Hmm," Commander Le'gon said. "Okay. But please explain how it relates to the numbers on the clock."

"Well, in the new way, enlightenment is the most important. Next would be to evolve. I feel my grandfather believed in science but thought we as the human race lost what was most important."

"And what would that be?" the commander asked.

"Well, religion, of course. Don't you see? Before, religion kept us in balance. There were rules to follow, such as not to lie or steal, and so on. Religion was a way for man to know where he stood and to understand where he failed. With religion, one would make their own conscious decision and know there would be a consequence if they went in the wrong direction."

The commander stood and paced the room. "Rachael, over time, millions of men have died because of religion. Over whose religion was right and whose was wrong. But who can prove there is an almighty God here to judge you in the end? There is no evidence to prove those claims. With the new way, man still has the ability to make conscious decisions. That is not dependent on the fear of being punished. And there is no longer war or greed. Now we're in pursuit of the truth."

"I understand, commander, but you're missing the most valued aspect of religion."

"And what would that be?"

"Faith. To have faith to step out and believe in oneself, and to have a greater cause. That is what we're missing today. We no longer have faith in ourselves."

Rachael knew she was risking a lot with that one sentence and worried she had made the wrong decision in seeking help.

"Faith, you say?" Commander Le'gon asked. "Do we not have faith in the Twelve? Does mankind not strive to make it to the final planet? What is it we think would be there?"

Their discussion really did feel like a lesson from her grandfather. She could tell the commander was angling for her to make up her own mind.

He asked, "What is the code to make the clock work and open the door?"

Rachael didn't hesitate to answer. "The hour hand represents religion, which represents that divinity will always be one.

Evolution is a constant, even when we as the human race stay still. This represents each minute that passes, which is the human—the number four. The second hand is the enlightened human, which represents the number five."

The commander was quiet for a long time. Finally, he said, "Rachael, thank you for coming and requesting assistance in this matter. Your grandfather had a brilliant mind, and it's a travesty that it was wasted. As you know, I came back to Planet Two to help shape the minds of the young, and your grandfather has given me my hardest task. My last question for you is if religion and faith are what we're missing, are you ready to lay down your life for the mere prospect of following your grandfather?"

Rachael felt sweat bead on her temple. "Commander, I don't understand your question."

"We left religion behind because it caused so many lives to be lost based on the faith that there was a divine being in the sky to wash away our sins. If your grandfather's new thought process returns us to the old ways, it could start a cycle we may not want to follow. So, are you willing to open that door? Are you willing to put your faith in your grandfather's hands and pursue an unknown path?"

"I don't know," she said.

There was an intensity in his eyes. She couldn't look away. "Rachael, the purpose of the Twelve is for the human mind to evolve, to enlighten ourselves beyond faith and know our destiny. Your grandfather left you a mighty inheritance, and it is up to you if you want it, but my judgment is that you are not ready for such a profound step in your life. I urge you not to go down this path. Continue on your own journey until you're surer of your course." Having passed his judgment, the commander exited the room.

Rachael couldn't believe it. She'd gone for help, but she was more confused than before. She tried to search for assurance deep inside, but something wasn't right. How could everything her grandfather taught her be wrong?

When she got home, Rachael mulled it over for a long time. She went back and forth. Her instincts told her not to do what her grandfather asked, to continue seeking enlightenment and circulation, but her curiosity and pride got the better of her. She liked that she would be able to shape her destiny by charting her own course.

She decided the commander didn't know her at all. Her grandfather had believed in her, and that was all she really needed. She would put the code into the clock, learn why her grandfather had made his choice, and decide from there how she would proceed.

Rachael turned each hand to the proper time, then opened the second door and pushed the rod to the side. She stood back and waited, trembling, not sure what to expect. As the rod swayed back and forth, she noticed the second hand start to spin around. Once it made a full rotation, the minute hand ticked to life. She watched it go all the way around, and then the hour hand moved.

Suddenly, there was a rush of wind, and the rod stopped mid swing. The bottom door popped open, but not enough for her to see inside. Rachael knew she needed to open it completely, but she was unable to move. It was the moment of truth. That one act could alter her entire life. She stepped closer to the clock, and after a moment of hesitation, she pulled the door open.

Abruptly, she was engulfed in silence. She squeezed her eyes shut, afraid. When nothing happened, she peeked through her eyelashes and saw complete whiteness. It was as if she were in a bubble, just like in the video of her grandfather.

His voice sounded behind her. "Hello, my dear, sweet girl!"

Rachael jumped and whirled around, her heart hammering so hard she couldn't hear herself breathe. He was there, smiling at her.

"Grandfather?" was all she could muster. A million thoughts went through her mind, but she couldn't turn them into words.

"I knew you would figure it out," he said. "I didn't think it would take you this long, but I am so proud of you. I knew you wouldn't let me down."

Rachael was still trying to calm her breathing. "Are... are you..." She waved her hand in the air, asking him to complete her sentence because she couldn't.

"Am I dead? Is that what you're trying to ask me?"

She nodded.

Her grandfather laughed. "Well, there is a complex answer to that. You see, my body and mind are well and alive. I'm just in a sort of stasis."

Rachael wanted to sit down, but there was nothing in the room. Or bubble, or whatever it was. "How am I seeing you?" she asked. "How am I talking to you? Did I die?"

"No, you are not dead. Per se."

"What does that mean, sir?"

Sir Benon grew serious. "My dear, what is the Golden Rule?"

That gave her pause. What did that have to do with anything?

When she didn't answer, he continued. "The Golden Rule states that the only thing that makes sense is to strive for greater collective enlightenment." He looked her in the eye to see if she comprehended his meaning. "My dear, in order for me to make it to Twelve, I need to achieve a greater *collective* enlightenment."

"What do you mean?" she asked in a quivering voice.

"Don't be slow, my dear. You know exactly what I mean. I raised you. I gave you lessons you should not have learned until you were more mature. Did you never wonder why?"

"So I could circulate early," Rachael said, though she feared that wasn't the real reason.

"No. You see, one can only gain so much knowledge on their own. To overcome that unfortunate limitation, Dlon Tung created a new technology to allow us to take the knowledge of others. To evolve. I elevated your mind to be a companion for mine."

Suddenly, Rachael understood and felt sick. "Are you saying all the people on Planet Twelve are killers? That everyone who makes it to Twelve has to trick someone in order to circulate?"

"'Killers' is a strong word, don't you think, my dear?"

That enraged her. "Don't you dare 'my dear' me! You had me born just so you could kill me to elevate yourself. 'Killers' is the proper word. In fact, it's the best word for the situation."

Sir Benon just watched her. Rachael had to find a way out. She had to stall him, keep him talking. She thought back to her conversation with Commander Le'gon.

"I spoke with a commander about the clock," she said. "He didn't tell me about any of this. Why wouldn't he warn me?" But Commander Le'gon had tried to dissuade her from opening the clock, she acknowledged to herself. Maybe that had been his warning.

A look of contempt crossed Sir Benon's face. "Commanders. Their kind make me sick. In my opinion, they should all be put to death."

"Why?" Rachael asked.

"Do you know the real reason people become commanders?"

Rachael shook her head.

"It's because when they learn the truth about how to reach Planet Twelve, they choose not to continue the journey. They're not willing to sacrifice another life for the betterment of mankind. Not willing to absorb another's knowledge to circulate. They claim the ticket for entry is too high a price, but they're just weak. They value their pathetic feelings over the collective enlightenment. They would never tell you the truth because they're too consumed by their guilt."

Rachael was shocked by his words. Sir Benon spoke of the betterment of humankind, but to her, it seemed the modern way of life was just as corrupt as religion.

"What was the point of the clock?" she asked, still hoping to stall him, to change his mind. "What was the point of being my teacher all these years if you were just going to kill me?"

Sir Benon shook his head in disgust. "I've already told you the point. I needed your mind to be elevated. I had to teach you so you would be worthy of becoming a part of me. The clock was your final test." He paused, momentarily distracted. "That reminds me, I must return it soon. It's long overdue."

Rachael could only stare at him. Return the clock? What did he mean? "I thought that was my inheritance."

He scoffed. "Inheritance. Why would I have such a useless thing? The clock was a test. A test to determine your willingness to lay down your life for the betterment of the worlds so I could fulfill my destiny as a Twelve. You should be proud of this moment. You should be honored."

"Lay down my life? I'm not laying down anything for you. You're a murderer, and I don't want any part of the Twelve. I hate you!"

He laughed, a booming roar. "Now you're acting like a child, and it is not becoming of you. And just so you understand, you already laid your life down for me the moment you opened that door. You chose your path. There is nothing left for you but to accept what is."

She knew in her heart he was telling the truth. She couldn't believe Dlon Tung, a person she'd admired her entire life, had helped shape the human race in such a manner. That it had been his image for man, his grand new world order. His passion for knowledge seemed sickening. Rachael decided everyone on Planet Twelve deserved each other.

She said, "You will have to live with the fact that you killed your own blood. That you elevated yourself on top of another precious human life."

For a moment, his eyes grew sad. She wondered if it was a show or if he actually felt some sort of regret for what he was doing to her. But even if he did, it made no difference. He still turned away from her and walked toward a door—a door that hadn't been there a moment ago.

"Will it hurt?" she asked.

He didn't answer. He didn't even look back. He went through the door and disappeared.

As Rachael was absorbed into his essence, she told herself she would still be there, that she was simply becoming a part of him. But in reality, she knew that who she truly was, Rachael herself as an individual, would be gone.

The last thing she felt was her mind wandering into an open space.

The End

About the Author

Shavona White

"I have always been curious about reality and my own purpose. At a very young age, I lost my father to a work accident, which led me to question life, death, and God. This often affects my sleep and causes anxiety. To cope and understand, I found solace in exploring others' thoughts through their art – books, movies, and more. I am passionate about individualism and what makes people unique. I observes patterns in people's behavior and their motivations. It is truly fascinating how one's environment shapes them, but others defy societal norms. I want to thank you for taking a journey through my mind and I hope you enjoyed it here.

Acknowledgments

I want to thank everyone who took the time to read my stories. Sharing my thoughts and putting them on paper was both difficult and fun.

I want to thank my formal writing club for the constructive feedback and encouragement to evolve and develop.

Connectiveness to a collective has always been difficult for me until I had my own family. I want to thank you all for always believing in me and putting up with my uniqueness.

I also want to thank my friends and, once again, my family for being supportive of my decision to put myself out there.

To anyone who struggles with the choices they make, try not to. Learn from your mistakes, learn from others' mistakes, and move on. When in the heat of the moment, you are the only one who can calm your brain to think through all possibilities.

Existentialism and psychology have been demonstrated in movies, books, art, and life. Try to take the time to understand and witness the beauty of making up your own mind.